Capitally Unexpected

RACHEL HOLM

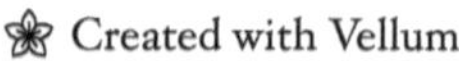 Created with Vellum

*For the people who feel like they have no idea what they're doing.
You're not alone. You'll make it through.*

Note from the Author

THANK you for picking up a copy of Capitally Unexpected! Hunter and Michelle were a joy to write, and I love how their story turned out.

As always, I like to include some content notes for anyone who feels they may benefit from them. This is especially true for this book, because it focuses so much on a person's pregnancy, which can be a difficult and sensitive subject for so many. I have attempted to portray all subjects mentioned below in a sensitive and responsible manner; any failure to do so lies with me alone. Please be gentle with yourself and take care while reading.

CONTENT NOTES INCLUDE:

External Fatphobia in Medicine (brief), negative body image discussion (brief); Death of parent (past, off page), Strained parental relationship (mother, past and present, on page); Pregnancy, Emergency Room trip during Pregnancy; Explicit content and language

CHAPTER
One

MICHELLE

"Listen, I don't normally do this, but . . ."

Has anything good in the history of the universe ever followed a sentence beginning that way? I rack my brain to think of an example not ending in disaster. I have plenty of time, since it seems to have slowed to a crawl. My leg bounces violently while I sit in the CVS bathroom down the street from my apartment waiting for the slowest three minutes of my whole life to pass.

This morning, I delivered a forecast of nothing but sunshine and blue skies for the weekend ahead. That reality feels a world away in this windowless bathroom smelling like the perfectly disgusting combination of chemicals and stale urine.

The timer on my phone rings in my hand causing me to throw the device face down onto the floor. "Fuck," I mutter, hoping my screen didn't crack. Though, depending on what's displayed on the stick resting on ten squares of folded toilet paper on top of the dispenser, a broken phone may be the least of my problems.

With a shaking hand and heartbeat in my ears, I reach to pick up the test, my gut twisting with anticipation. And there on the screen reads the word I've been expecting since I realized this morning my not-so-regular period is late. Really late. *Pregnant.*

"Fuck," I mutter again, wrapping the stick in more toilet paper and shoving it back into the box I ripped clean in half in my haste to get it open. I take a moment to try to slow my breathing, taking in a few deep breaths. Picking my phone off the floor and shoving everything into my tote bag, I emerge from the stall. I stare at the woman in the mirror while I wash my hands in a daze.

Michelle Lewis. Natural Redhead. Meteorologist. Lover of Margaritas and Karaoke.

And . . . Mother?

I emerge from the bathroom with a determined stride. As a scientist, we never trust the results of only one test. Marching to the aisle where the pregnancy tests hang mockingly next to the packs of condoms, I snatch five more brands off their hooks. I grab a box of condoms with the recognizable black packaging. When I flip it over, the words seem to jump off the back despite their fine print: up to ninety-eight percent effective.

"What a time to be a member of the two percent," I mutter, before spiking the box onto the bottom of the display. Guilt runs through me, so I lean down to pick up the offending cardboard and hang it on the hook. It's not some poor CVS employee's fault I haven't found a new doctor since my move to Washington DC and let my birth control prescription lapse. Nope, this is between me, a magnum-sized penis, and my, apparently, overripe uterus.

At the last minute, I tuck the pack of condoms into the pile of pregnancy tests in my arms. It might come in handy to have that disclaimer in print over the next few months.

I arrive at the front of the store, groaning internally when I see the self-checkouts are out of order. When it's my turn, I place my boxes carefully on the counter and look everywhere except at the cashier ringing me out.

"You'd be surprised how often these items get purchased together, sweetie," the kind older woman scanning my purchases says. Her tone is gentle and strikes a chord inside me, one that makes me realize this is real. This is happening.

"Yeah?" I say, wincing at the wobble in my voice. "Do they ever come back to let you know which one was the more necessary purchase?"

She chuckles softly. "Why don't you be my first?" She holds my bag out to me while I press my card to the machine.

"I might just do that." The idea of sharing my news with this kind stranger feels easier than telling my cousin, my friends, or god forbid, my mom. The father . . . is a shitstorm I don't want to consider until I know my next move.

I check my phone leaving the store, a smile crossing my face despite the weight pushing down on my shoulders. My friend Jax and her boyfriend—fake fiancé? Whatever you wanted to call him!—Preston have made up. I type out a message letting her know I'm not moving another box, but I'm happy for her.

My hand instinctively goes to my stomach as I walk down the street, barely noticing the sunshine and blue skies I had so accurately forecast a few hours ago. Even though I'm carrying a bag full of backup tests, I know in my gut they'll all say the same thing. I pull my phone out again, this time to start making a list. Among the doctor's appointments and topics to research goes a Tinder handle belonging to a man who has strayed into my thoughts more often than I'd like to admit over the last eight weeks. Ridgeman93.

CHAPTER
Two

HUNTER

Eight weeks earlier

I check the address on my phone with the one hanging above the doorway in front of me. Cupping my hand in front of my face, I do a quick breath check. More minty fresh than scotch laced. To be safe, I shove another piece of gum into my mouth from the pack I grabbed at the CVS down the street, chewing quickly. A garbage can to the right of the entrance catches my eyes. After checking left and right to be sure no one is around, I pull the three-pack box of condoms I also grabbed at CVS out of the paper bag. Box, bag, receipt, and gum thrown in the trash can and foil packages safely deposited in my wallet, I buzz for 2D. Home of Weathergirl85.

"Hello?" A voice crackles on the intercom.

"Uh, hey. It's me. You know, from Tin—"

"Yup, got it! Come on up." The voice cuts me off in a rush as the door buzzes, letting me in. I chuckle to myself, glad I'm not the only one a little nervous about this situation. While I'm no stranger to hookups back home in Holly Ridge, it's a little out of my comfort zone to meet a woman in a strange city when I'm supposed to be visiting my twin, Hayden. I opened Tinder on a whim earlier today. Surrounded by two of my brothers with their partners had me feeling a bit lonely. Right before I closed the app, not wanting those same brothers to give me hell, or worse, offer to help with swiping, a message came through. A cloud of wavy auburn hair covered a woman's face, the ends of the strands pointing directly to one hell of a cleavage show, peaking out of a jewel green top.

"So, I assume the Ridge refers to your abs? Because I think you could see those from space." The first message read. Then a second after. "God, that was awful. I might as well send you a picture of me holding a fish, followed by an unsolicited dick pic. I'm way out of my element here."

"Consider me that fish, because I'm hooked." I wrote back, and we were off from there. I've been so focused on school and work the last few months, so it's been a while since my last hookup. Not having to listen to my brother and his girlfriend try to muffle their moans from across the hall for a second night in a row is a fringe benefit.

A deep breath in and I'm knocking on the door. After a second, it opens slowly, revealing a fucking specimen of a woman. The auburn waves and cleavage from the photo are present, but now I can take in the sparkling blue eyes, the freckles splashed across her cheeks, and the curve of her waist.

"Hi."

"Hi," I say back, still in the hall with my hands shoved into my pockets.

"Um, I guess you should come in." She steps aside so I can walk into her apartment. "I feel like you should know my cousin knows you're here right now, and we may not know your name, but she has screenshots of your profile. Pretty identifiable features." She gestures to the tattoo sleeves covering my arms, running up under my shirt sleeves.

"Well, that's just good sense. My brother knows I'm here too.

Well, not necessarily *here* here, but he knows I'm meeting up with someone."

"Glad we're both being safe," she says, continuing to stand right inside the door. I take the opportunity to look around her apartment, not wanting to rush her. It's cozy and welcoming with splashes of color coming from intentionally chosen decorations and photos. The result is neat and organized, not cluttered.

"Listen, I don't normally do this," she says, her skin flushing under those freckles I can see myself becoming obsessed with.

"What, stand in your entryway with a strange man?" I tease gently, hoping to break the tension.

"Do anything with strange men." She brings her hand up to palm her face. "God, that makes it sound like I'm living in *Bridgerton* or something. I've obviously been around men I don't know before, but not typically in my home, having been invited explicitly for sex, after knowing nothing about them except they're susceptible to corny pickup lines."

"It was cute," I say while walking slowly toward her, making my intentions obvious. "But I have to say, now that I'm here, cute isn't the right word. Sexy, devastating, enchanting. Take your pick."

Her eyes open wide as I come to a stop in front of her, tucking a strand of hair behind her ear. "But if you want me to go, say the word and I will."

My offer seems to unlock something in her eyes, her mouth taking on a sly slant. "I would like you to go . . . down on me."

I bark out a laugh of surprise, which causes a smile to take over her face, her eyes sparkling brighter. "It would be my pleasure. Do you want it right here, against the door? Or would you prefer a bed?"

She mulls it over for a moment before pushing on my shoulder to spin me around, giving me a gentle push in the direction of the hallway ahead of us. "Bedroom. Door on the left. I'll be right there."

I walk down the hallway as my host ducks into a doorway off

to the right and shuts the door behind her. More artwork and photos catch my eye, but I don't want to ignore instructions, so I keep moving until I'm in her bedroom. The only light comes from a lamp next to the bedside table. The lampshade is a dark color, throwing muted sepia tones across the room. My shoes are still on, so I toe them off inside the door. If this were one of my regular, well formerly regular, hookups at home, I'd probably wait for them naked on the bed. Something tells me that's not WeatherGirl's style. Besides, she seems like she needs a release, and I intend to give her as many as she'll let me.

A few more minutes pass with me standing next to her bed, and I wonder if she's getting cold feet. I untuck my shirt from my jeans and take the condoms out of my wallet. Should I put them on the bed? The table next to the lamp? Is she ever coming out of that bathroom or do I not need to worry about condom placement at all?

The bathroom door creaks open and I drop the foil packets onto the bedside table out of panic.

Her shadow enters the room first, drawing my eyes to the floor. Bare feet with pink polish appear and my eyes follow a trail up to discover naked shins, then naked thighs. My heart rate picks up as my eyes touch on the jewel green lace, a similar color to the shirt in her Tinder photo, making up the bottom of the sheer body suit she wears. It hugs every curve over her hips and stomach, the V between her breasts pointing low and angling wide, showing off a pair of fantastic tits. By the time my eyes reach her face, she's leaning against the doorjamb with a knowing smile. A hint of pink tinges her cheeks from my perusal.

"Wow," I start. "You look . . . I mean, just . . . that color with your hair, and the . . . well, your tits—"

"Look insane, right?" She finishes my sentence word for word, which snaps me out of the trance her sudden appearance put me in.

A growl emits deep from my throat, and I cross the room in

a few strides. One hand wraps around to her lower back and I bury the other in her hair. "I'd very much like to kiss you now." I grit out, warring between wanting to devour her whole, but making sure she's on board with being consumed.

"Yes, please," she breathes, and then my mouth is on hers. A groan reverberates in my chest as she matches my enthusiasm, working my mouth open with her tongue and tangling it with mine. Her hands pull on my short blond hair, the roots of which seem to be routed straight to my groin, as my hips thrust into her. She moans into my mouth, releasing the strands and sliding her hands along my shoulders to the front of my shirt. It appears multitasking is a strength of hers, as she brings her mouth to kiss on my neck while undoing the buttons.

"Shit . . . No, don't stop," I say, when she pauses her work after my curse. "I . . . I don't even know your name."

Her hands pause on the final button holding my shirt together. They rest above where I'm rock hard, testing the restraint of the denim of my jeans. She looks up at me with appraising eyes.

"You said you don't live in the city?"

"No, I'm visiting family. Here for the weekend."

"Then what about no names? You be RidgeMan and I'll be WeatherGirl. Or Bonnie and Clyde. Whatever works for you."

I wink at her, even as my heart sinks. Realization I'll never know the whole self of this vixen setting in. "Be sure you don't steal my heart, Bonnie." Not that I'm sure there's anything in my heart worth stealing.

"Who says I'm Bonnie?" she says, winking right back. The final button comes free, and she pushes my shirt off my shoulders until it falls to the floor. Her hands run over the colorful tattoos covering my arms onto my shoulders, the edges of the sleeves ending below my collarbone. "These are gorgeous."

"Why thank you, Clyde," I say with a smirk, which only grows when she smiles up at me. "Now I believe I promised you something on this bed here. I try to keep my word, especially to my partner in crime." Accountability hasn't always been my strong suit, but I've been working on myself these past eighteen months, so it almost doesn't feel like a lie when the words leave my mouth.

She walks over to the bed, giving me the first view of the high cut of lace laying across her luscious ass cheeks. I think about how the color spread across her chest earlier and wonder how her ass would look tinged a little pink from my hand. With her permission, of course.

Clyde settles against the ample pillows scattered across the top of her bed. I follow her path, popping the button and pulling down the zipper on my jeans to provide my cock a little breathing room. Kneeling next to her on the bed, I take her mouth in another deep kiss before kissing my way down her body. I bite at her nipples through the lace, taking pleasure in how she arches her back and moans.

"So responsive," I say against the lace and skin of her stomach before I bend each of her legs so her feet lie flat on the bed. Her knees part under my hands to make room for my broad shoulders. My fingers slip under the band of lace covering her pussy. The back of my knuckles brush against her wet slit.

"Well, that's convenient," I murmur, spotting the two clasps holding the the body suit together. Checking in with my weather girl, I make my intentions clear and wait for her nod before directing my eyes back at her center. Pulling apart the clasps, her pussy comes into view. I lean down to lick from her entrance to her clit, groaning at the taste.

"You sure do taste like sin, Clyde. No wonder you turned to a life of crime." She giggles before threading her fingers through my hair. I take the hint and get to work.

CHAPTER
Three

MICHELLE

This isn't my life. This must be something out of a dream, because there is no way this beautiful, tattooed man is between my legs, letting me call him Bonnie, and eating me like he's trying to find the center of a Tootsie pop.

"Fuck," I yell, my hips arching off the bed as he slaps my clit sharply before licking the sting away. If I were sleeping, the mix of pleasure and pain would have woken me up in an instant.

"Just making sure you're still with me. You're holding back on my sounds." As if on cue, a noise I'm certain I've never made before rips from my throat while he twirls his tongue and angles his fingers in unison. "Better," he says, chuckling darkly. The vibrations from his laugh thrum through my core.

I prop myself up on one elbow, wanting to commit the sight to memory. My other hand is tight in his hair, making sure he finishes what he started. He seems content to complete the mission or die trying. His painted arms hold down my legs as they threaten to squeeze against the pleasure. He adds one more finger to his thrusts before sucking my clit into his mouth with the perfect pressure to tip me over the edge. My view goes hazy, and my arm gives out, my back meeting the bed. He continues to work me through the waves of pleasure. The fingers tangled in his hair loosen their grip once I come down to earth. The next second, I tighten them again to tug him away from my core, too sensitive to bear anymore. Bonnie moves away immediately, climbing up my body so his gaze meets mine. He groans and I glance down to see the tip of his cock peeking out above his boxer briefs, dragging along the lace covering my stomach. He shivers from the sensation. I want to make him shiver again.

"Hi," he says, his eyes hot on mine as his tongue licks in a circle, tasting the proof of the most intense orgasm of my life from his lips.

"Hu—hi," I huff out, still finding myself short on breath. It should be awkward, having a near stranger boxing me in, no words passing between us. Instead, I take comfort in our physical compatibility. To think of all those years I wasted believing I couldn't remove the emotion from sex. I hadn't tried hard enough. Not knowing their name! Can't get less emotionally connected than that.

"So," he says, still hovering over me. "Anything else on your to-do list this evening?" His voice carries a tone indicating I'm still completely in charge here. If I told him to leave, he would, facing the risk of an indecent exposure charge. I'm not sure he's going to get that massive dick back into his pants without a little assistance or a lot of pain.

It hits me, along with leaving the ball in my court, he's essentially been holding a plank over my body for at least a minute. I'd love to see what else his core strength can do.

"I can think of an item or two . . . hundred we can accomplish before dawn," I say, teasing my fingers up his bicep. Perceptive may as well be his middle name. He reads my mind and flips us over so I'm straddling his waist, his cock greeting the crack of my ass from this position.

"Item one is getting both of us a bit more naked," I say,

unsure who this one-night stand sex goddess is, but hoping she sticks around after the night is over. I pull the lace up over my head, unable to stop the groan as the texture slides over my nipples. His hands immediately move to cover the newly exposed skin, tweaking and massaging the hard peaks. "You're distracting me from my goals," I tease, leaning down to tangle my tongue with his before sliding further down his body.

I grip the waist of his underwear and jeans and, with a helpful tilt of his hips, yank them to his thighs in one motion. His cock slaps his stomach with the sudden removal of the restraining fabric. "I'm coming back for you," I say as I work his jeans the rest of the way off, my eyes never leaving where his tip is dark and leaking. Keeping my promise, I circle my hand around his base, marveling at the gap between my fingers. We're going to have to take this slow and steady.

I lean down and take as much of him as I can in my mouth. "Fuck, Clyde, I knew your mouth would feel like heaven," Bonnie groans. His head tips back in the pillows while my hand shuttles up and down on the part of his cock my mouth can't take. Remembering how much I liked the surprise of him slapping my clit, I move one hand down to cradle his balls, before pushing a finger against the skin below. His hips jerk up, his cock hitting the back of my throat. My eyes water as I pull off.

"Fuck, I'm sorry," he breathes, reaching a hand down to cradle my cheek. "You caught me off guard there."

"Note to self," I say, wiping under my eyes with the corner of my comforter, smiling to let him know I'm okay. "Make sure you can swallow the sword before antagonizing the one feeding it to you."

He laughs, a deep husky sound. It fills the emptiness left after a hard conversation with my boss earlier today. Who I am *not* thinking about during this very out of character, casual hook up. The idea Bonnie's laugh has any power over me feels dangerous.

"You okay?" he asks, the hand on my cheek moving to stroke

my arm. This tips me off my demeanor change showed on the outside too.

"Yup," I say, shaking my hair over my shoulder before leaning down, hovering over his cock once more. "Just preparing myself." With that, I return to work, not trying any more surprise hand movements, but focusing on the basics. Bonnie doesn't seem to have any complaints, the strain in his abs betraying the effort he's putting in to not thrusting. His hand tangles in my hair as his eyes stay locked on where I'm taking him in and out of my mouth.

Right as the tip of his cock hits the back of my throat, on purpose this time, he yanks on my hair. My mouth pulls off with a pop, and his cock smacks his stomach once more.

"So-sorry," he says, his hand reaching down to grip tightly around the base of his dick, his eyes scrunched tight trying to stop from coming. "That snuck up on me."

I smirk. "So, you didn't bring those condoms for decoration, then?" I nod toward the foil packets that appeared on the nightstand while I changed in the bathroom.

"They don't really go with the rest of the aesthetic in your room, but I like to come prepared."

"Such a good little Boy Scout," I say, leaning over to reach for one of the foil packets. He lets out a sardonic laugh before taking it from me. Ripping the packet open with his teeth, he rolls it on his substantial length. "I think I lasted about three weeks in the Boy Scouts before they asked my dad to not bring me back with my twin the next week." Something flashes in his eyes, but it's gone in an instant, replaced with a smirk and smolder. "Good thing 'Be Prepared' is lesson number one." He holds his cock up for me as I hover over him.

"Good thing indeed," I say. Lowering myself slowly, the tip of cock stretches me wide. Maybe being on top isn't my brightest decision. I work myself down bit by bit, relishing the way his hands grip my hips.

"God, you're like a vice," he says, tightening his grip to match his words as I bottom out. "Need to move," he says a moment later, the words spoken behind gritted teeth. "You okay?"

I answer by lifting myself up slightly and his instinct kicks in, helping to guide my hips up slowly before lowering me back down. We move at this slow and steady pace for a few thrusts until my thighs begin to burn with the effort of my restrained movements.

"Bonnie?" I say, shifting to lean over him, my nipples sensitive as they drag against his chest. His eyes shift up from where they were watching him enter me to meet mine.

"Yeah, Clyde?" he says as he drags out another slow thrust, causing my clit to meet his pubic bone in the most delicious way.

"Pound me." My cheeks warm. "Please," I add, pulling my gaze from his, focusing on the pillow below his head as uncertainty washes over me.

He releases my hip and cups my cheek, urging me to meet his eyes, before shifting to the back of my neck and pulling my head down to his. This kiss starts sweet and reassuring before our tongues are fucking and I find myself grinding down onto his dick.

He releases me, his smile wicked as he responds. "Gladly."

His next thrust reaches new depths and I gasp as he takes over the pace. His hands take hold of my hips again in a way I almost hope leaves a mark. That core strength shows up in his hard thrusts and furious pace, each one dragging my clit against him again and again. I climb and climb before turning my head to scream into a pillow a second before falling off the cliff. He continues to thrust as my pussy milks his cock, slowing down in time with the waves of pleasure distancing themselves from my shore.

I lay there draped on him as he caresses my bare skin, all the while slowly rolling his hips up into me. As I come back to myself, I realize he's still incredibly hard. My hips start to roll in time with his again, sparks flying where I was boneless seconds ago.

He takes this as a cue and flips me onto my back and holding himself over my body.

"Look at us," he growls, directing my attention to where he's thrusting in and out of me, his silicone-covered cock slick with my release. "You take me so well."

I groan at the filth of his words, how they reverberate inside me. I once had a vast vocabulary of words, capable of explaining complex weather forecasts and discussing the merits of which Real Housewives cast reigns supreme. Now, I'm reduced to single words. "More. Fuck. Please. Yes."

His pace picks up. "You keep looking there if you want. I'm going to watch you. You robbed me of watching you while you came on my dick last time. So, I'm going to need you to give me one more."

Like a clap of rolling thunder, my orgasm rises again. Bonnie's hips thrust with enough force the headboard knocks on the wall, leaving me grateful for my exterior facing bedroom. I bite my lip before he reaches to roughly pull it out from between my teeth, leaving a sting behind.

"Don't you dare keep those sounds from me. I want to hear you."

There's only so much a girl can take, and I detonate around him. His rhythm stutters, once, twice, before thrusting deep and staying there, riding out his own release. His arms give out and he drops his full weight on me before rolling to the side, bringing me with him. In a tangle of limbs and sweat covered bodies, we press together as we catch our breaths.

"You know, I just didn't want to blow your ear drum out," I say after a few moments of heavy breathing in the otherwise quiet room.

"The fact you were able to make a conscious choice in the moment sets my bar for next time," he says, his fingers brushing along my spine.

"Next time?" I ask, moving in a way that causes his softening cock to pull out. I try to hide my wince, but his furrowed brow tells me I failed.

"You said something about dawn, didn't you?" He turns his head to take in the clock next to my bed. It reads a little after ten. "I'd say we have a ways to go before first light. Let me take care of this"—he gestures to his dick—"and grab you a cloth to clean up and we'll discuss next time."

I roll onto my back, still not fully believing this is a real-life entry in my timeline. "In that case, I'm going to need a snack," I mutter, mostly to myself.

He pulls on his boxer briefs after dropping the tied off condom in the trash can. "Cloth first, and then if it's okay, I'll raid your kitchen and see what I can pull together."

As he leaves the room, I call after him. "Only if you promise to not put anymore clothes on while you do it."

He gladly adheres to my request, after making one of his own: I'm only putting my robe on to allow him to focus. I'm surprised at how much we talk and laugh while he makes the most delicious post-sex egg scramble I've ever had. He takes me back to bed, making good on his promise to put me completely out of my mind before we fall into an exhausted sleep in the early morning hours.

I wake up to bright sunshine streaming through the window of the blinds I never closed last night. The sheets next to me are cold to the touch, twisting my stomach into a knot I didn't expect. I'm sure in my gut the apartment is empty. Still, I find myself peeking into the bathroom before wandering into an equally unoccupied living area. A piece of paper on the counter catches my eye, the messy handwriting unfamiliar.

Clyde,

Sorry to let you wake up by yourself. I worried if I waited, I wouldn't be able to stop myself from asking for your real name and your phone number. But that's not what you said you wanted. If you change your mind, you know where to find me.

Forever your partner in sexy crime,
Bonnie

I sit on the stool next to the island, my memories tripping over last night. I can at least send him a message to be sure he got home okay. Or, what's to stop us from meeting up when he's in town again in the future? I search for my phone and right on cue, two quick vibrations in a row fill the space. It's lying face up on the coffee table. I pick it up with the intention of opening Tinder, but my most recent email notification distracts me instead. It's an email from my boss, requesting a meeting first thing tomorrow morning. He wants to follow up on the conversation we had before I left on Friday about the "overly technical" nature of my forecasts.

With that, the bubble is broken. I've put years into my career, sacrificing my social life, boyfriends, and countless other things along the way. There isn't any time to lose focus now. I pick up my phone again and navigate to Tinder. The message thread with RidgeMan93 opens, but I force myself to close out of it. I navigate through the menus, my thumb hovering over the screen for a few seconds before I confirm I want to deactivate my account. After I delete the app, I shove my phone in the couch cushions, wanting it out of sight and out of mind.

Okay, Michelle. One hour of wallowing in a bath to soothe your aching body, and then no more thinking about why your body feels so deliciously used.

I push up off the couch and push through the wave of sadness that hits me. Goodbye, RidgeMan.

HUNTER

2 months later

I'm not one for pomp and circumstance, yet the song blares over the speakers at Winterberry Glen's community college as I walk down the aisle toward the front rows reserved for the graduates. Midway down, a wolf whistle cuts through the crowd noise, causing everyone around me in line to look to the left.

Cheers of "Hunter! Woo! Go Brandt!" erupt from the section we're walking past. My cheeks heat as my four brothers, two of their partners, my dad, and my stepmom take up almost a whole row of their own. A warmth a lot like pride and maybe a bit like embarrassment takes up residence in my chest.

My brothers hold nine college and post-graduate degrees between them, and I worried the ceremony at a community college wouldn't hold up to all those events. So far though, everything seems to be the same. Big song, graduates walking in lines wearing caps and gowns, and now, the start of a revolving stage of speeches. My mind starts to wander, heading where it always does these days.

To a night almost two months ago. My weather girl, with her contagious laugh, quick sense of wit, and well, yes, her bangin' body. The way she moaned as I slid into her for the third time, gripping that ass . . .

An elbow in my side jolts me into awareness as a voice booms from the stage. "Now presenting, the graduates for the degree of Associates in Culinary Arts." I stand up, catching up with the rest of my class. Never thought I'd be glad for the shape of a graduation gown, but not having to worry if you can see my half-chub in these photos is a huge a relief.

I jolt back into the moment. Sentimental isn't a word many would use to describe me, but I know what a big deal today is, not only for me, but for my family who has been waiting a good long time for me to grow up.

Being so close to the front of the alphabet means I don't have wait long before I hear "Hunter Brandt," from the same booming voice. I walk forward a few steps and grab my diploma from some dude and shake hands with more women and men I'm maybe supposed to know. At graduation rehearsal, they hammered home we're supposed to turn around and stop for our official photo. I rolled my eyes then, but when the man with the camera frantically waves his hands to get my attention, I realize they probably know what they're talking about.

I put on a grin for the camera. The whole row of my family explodes in a standing ovation. My smile gets a lot bigger, and I blink back a few tears as they continue to cause a huge scene. Not wanting to blubber in front of all these people, I hit a strong man pose. It gets a huge laugh from the crowd. I jog down the stairs to head to my seat, smile still pulling at my cheeks. Maybe I don't have to grow all the way up right now.

The parking lot is a sea of black gowns and proud family members as I wander through, looking for my people. While I search, I nod at a few faces I recognize from my classes, racking my brain for their names. Maybe I should have made more of an effort to connect with my peers. I still need to secure a job with this culinary arts degree we're making such a big deal about, and I always hear my oldest brother Duncan talking about networking.

Whooping from my right pulls me out of those thoughts as a whole crowd of Brandts stand next to a landscaping island with colorful flowers soaking up the late spring sun. My twin, Hayden, is the first one to pull me into a hug. His back pats may be a bit harder than necessary.

"Proud of you, Hunt," he says, his voice a little rough as he pulls back to let everyone else have their turn. My dad isn't trying to hide the tears in his eyes and gratefully takes the tissue my stepmom, Margaret, holds out for him.

After everyone has gotten their hugs in, we stand in a circle. Awkwardness starts to settle over me when Hayden's girlfriend, Charlotte, breaks the silence. "Hey now, Jax and I didn't fight people off for this prime photo spot to stand here! Let's Kodak this moment!"

Everyone jumps into action as Margaret shepherds us into position. She may have married my dad when Hayden and I were seventeen, but she's a natural at managing our circus.

"Thanks," I mutter to Charlotte in the transition.

"Don't mention it," she says. "Your trapped face is the same as Hayden's." I open my mouth, and she holds up a hand, cutting me off. "No, I do not wonder what other faces you may share, nor do I want to find out."

I laugh, hooking her arm around mine for a moment before handing her off to my twin. They save the spot in the middle of the group for me.

"I can take it," Jax, Preston's partner, says, pulling her phone out of her bag and making motions to leave her spot by Preston.

"My assistant was supposed to come this weekend so we could avoid this moment and act as photographer, but she had a *family situation*," Duncan says with ire, ignoring the irony of being involved in a family situation of his own right now. I meet the eyes of my second oldest brother, Preston, before matching his eye roll. We'll have to get another pool going to see how long it is before Duncan fires this one.

"No way," Margaret says. "We need to get the whole family in." I watch Preston kiss Jax's cheek, flushed a rosy pink.

"Yoohoo, excuse me! Can one of you take our picture?" Margaret waves down a family next to us. "We'll gladly do the same for you when we're done."

We fumble with whose phone the picture should be on, before all agreeing Charlotte is the most responsible to remember to share it with everyone. Photo ownership settled, my family tightens in around me, yelling cheese when prompted. The warmth in my chest returns. My brothers all have lives and high-powered jobs. Hell, our youngest brother, Spencer, only gets like five days a year off from his lab. But here we all are together for the first time in forever, and they came together for me.

I listen to Spencer and Preston argue about some nuclear energy bill being proposed in Congress as Margaret stage manages another family into a successful group photo.

"So, we have that reservation at Joe's Café for dinner. Everyone still coming?" my dad asks.

Preston and Jax exchange a look. "We're so sorry, but Senator Marsden needs us to drive over to Rhode Island and meet him tonight, ahead of an event tomorrow. He put it on our schedule yesterday."

Duncan looks at this phone, curses, and shakes his head. "I'm out too. Something's up with the Asian markets and I need to look at this before we have a major crash on our hands."

The warmth slowly seeps out of me, even though I understand. The fact we were all in one place on a non-holiday is a feat.

"Well, I can't wait for some sangria and a cheeseburger as big as my head," Spencer says, clapping his hand on my shoulder.

"We'll be there too," Hayden says. "We're staying with Charlotte's parents tonight, but they don't expect us until late."

I smile gratefully at them.

"Okay, hugs before those of you leaving hit the road, please," Margaret says with a proud smile. "Everyone else, we'll see you in thirty minutes."

As Duncan releases me from a hug, he grips my shoulder. "I'm really sorry I have to go, Hunt. There is something I want to talk to you about, but I think it'll have to wait. Why don't you come to DC for Memorial Day weekend, and we'll do it then?"

"Awesome, something to obsess over for a few weeks," I say, rolling my eyes, but softening it with a smile.

"It's good news, I promise. At least, I think it is. I'll have Brenda arrange the details," he says, turning to walk to his car, his face already buried in his phone.

"You fired Brenda two months ago," Hayden yells after him, his arm around my shoulder. His body shakes with laughter against my side when Duncan flips him off from two rows away.

"All right, mister culinary man," he says, yanking on the corner of the cap I somehow forgot I'm still wearing. "Let's go let our parents pay for our food. Nothing says fresh college graduate more than that."

"Community college," I say, not sure why I add the qualifier.

He spins around in front of me, bracketing me on both shoulders. "Hey man, don't do that. You set a goal, and you accomplished it. School isn't going to be everyone's thing, and community colleges are a backbone of workforce preparedness. Be proud of yourself."

"Thanks, Hay," I say.

"Anytime." Changing focus, he shouts, "I call shotgun," and runs off toward Dad and Margaret's SUV.

I shake my head, following to drop off my cap and gown before I get on my bike to ride over to dinner. Maybe I'm not the only one who still hasn't grown all the way up.

CHAPTER

Five

MICHELLE

Ten weeks pregnant

I shift in the uncomfortable olive-green chair, wincing in the fluorescent lighting. The waiting room of this OBGYN office doesn't look much different from the ones I've sat in the rest of my life. Except this is the first time I need the services of the "OB" part of the acronym.

"Are you okay? Do you need anything?" My friend Jax asks from the burnt orange chair next to me. What does it mean I chose the green chair over the orange one? Green radar means light rain, maybe only a drizzle. Orange radar means shit is about to get very real, very fast. An orange chair is more appropriate for my current life stage.

"No, I'm fine." I look at my phone to check the time, again. "I hope they call me back soon. I know things happen, but it took me two weeks to get an appointment early enough I could come before I need to be at the station." The weird hours of local weather news don't always line up with things like normal business hours.

I glance over at the to-do list Jax is working on. "You don't have to wait, you know. I know this is one of your off days from the senator's office. You must have a million things to get done." Jax recently had the secret pen name she writes romance under exposed. Long story short, her career has exploded, and I'm positive she has better things to do than sitting here with me.

"I'm not going anywhere." Jax fixes me with a stare that would stand a chance of stopping an avalanche. "You'd be here alone right now if I hadn't walked in on you staring at your bouquet of pregnancy tests when I came back for my laptop charger. Admit it."

She has me there. "I might have told Laurel . . ." I trail off, my tone unconvincing. My cousin will probably try to make me move in with her and her wife to keep an eye on me. I need to have a plan in place before she learns anything.

"Sure, Jan," Jax snorts, confirming I don't fool her. "And even if you had, she'd be in Marsden's office right now anyway. So, I'm pretty much the best woman for the job."

"Lewis!" My name being called from the door leading to the exam rooms saves me from considering if I'm the best woman for this job—motherhood.

"Are you sure you don't want me to come back with you?" While Jax insisted on coming to the appointment, she is respecting me not wanting anyone in the exam room with me. I have to admit, knowing she's here helps more than I can put into words.

"No, I'm gonna be alone for a lot of these appointments, so let's start now," I say, hefting my bag with my notebook full of questions for the doctor onto my shoulder.

"Go team!" Jax yells from her seat, and I turn around to see her encouraging smile. Taking a deep breath, I walk past the pink-scrubbed nurse holding the door open.

"Stop here so we can get your height and weight." She's all business, pointing to where I can set my bag. I step up on the scale. As she moves the sliders around, I make a mental note to add setting up more frequent appointments with my therapist to the list. I've come to terms that I need to stand up for myself when it comes to doctors and my weight. Even so, watching the numbers slowly creep up, should this pregnancy move forward, is something I'll want support handling.

The numbers are recorded in my chart, and I follow her to a white room with an exam table, some machines with screens, and a couple of chairs near a desk. The nurse indicates I should sit in a chair first.

She goes over the health history information I provided at digital check-in. "And the first day of your last period was?" I give her the date from my Health app. She nods as she types it into the computer. "And you've gotten a positive result on a home pregnancy test?"

"About twelve of them," I say, noticing she's trying to hold back a smile. "I know, I know," I continue. "I wanted to be . . . sure."

She nods. "All right, the doctor will be in shortly. One more thing, I see there's no partner's name in the file?"

I've been dreading this part. "That's correct. It wasn't immaculate conception, but the partner won't be in the picture." She keeps a professional straight face, but I pick out pity in her eyes. I wonder how often she sees a woman coming in here alone.

"Well, you're seeing Dr. Barber today—she's a great one for your first visit." Her voice projects compassion and kindness, the businesslike tone from earlier gone.

"Thank you so much . . . I'm so sorry. I'm sure you told me your name, but it didn't stick." She smiles, a genuine smile that comes from someone noticing you.

"I'm Christina," she says.

"Michelle," I say, indicating myself. "I think you'll be seeing a lot of me."

She laughs. "I think you might be right."

She slips out of the room and leaves me to my thoughts. Pretty much the last place I want to be these days. It's why my list of questions is so long. If I'm researching or learning something, then I'm not spinning out, worrying if I can do this. If I *want* to do this.

I dig in my bag for a pencil. Not finding one, I decide to snoop to see if there's one I can borrow. Not spotting anything on top of the desk and still left to my own devices, I decide to try the drawer. It's stuck, damn it. I give it one more yank, pulling it right off its track, and about a dozen speculums spill all over the floor right as the door opens and Dr. Barber, I assume, walks in.

"Hi," I say, holding the drawer in my right hand, positive my skin is flushing.

"Eager to get started? I'm Dr. Barber." The woman, who's not much older than me walks the rest of the way into the room and crouches down with me to start picking up the metal pieces from the floor.

"I'm so sorry. I forgot to put a pen in my bag and thought maybe there'd be one in the desk and . . ."

She puts a hand on my arm, a kind smile on her face. "It's okay. This is nowhere near the weirdest thing I've walked into in a patient room."

"Well, fuck HIPAA, because that's a story I'd love to hear," I say as I sit back in my chair.

"It's one I would love to tell you, but even without my confidentiality requirements, you work in a news station. I'm not sure you would be a good confidant." My eyebrows shoot up, surprised she recognizes me.

"I've been watching KUSN for years and was thrilled when they hired a female meteorologist. And one who knows her science and isn't afraid to show it? Well, you're a weather woman after this scientist's heart."

"Wow, I'm just so surprised you recognized me. It hasn't happened a ton yet. I haven't been there very long. Of course, the first time it happens . . ."

"Is when you're meeting the woman who's very shortly going

to get between your legs." She winks, somehow knowing the perfect bedside manner to match my vibes in a few short moments. And for the first time since I peed on that stick in CVS, I can see a path forward. I only need to be willing to grab it. Dr. Barber, angel sent from heaven, is here to help guide me.

"All right, let's get down to it. The test from the urine sample you provided when you arrived came back positive, as expected. You are pregnant."

All the air leaves my body, the momentary calm fleeing like I'm a whoopee cushion and Dr. Barber sat right on me.

"I see you're in the room on your own. Will anyone be joining you for future appointments?"

"My friend Jax is out in the waiting room, but no. I very much expect to be in this room on my own."

Her perfunctory nod is all business and contains no judgment, which is a huge relief. "Okay, I'll make a note, so you don't get asked anymore. Assuming you decide to continue returning for these appointments."

Her tone indicates she's not referring to finding another practice. One page of my notebook is dedicated to this, but as I continued to fill up the other pages with additional subjects and questions, that one page stayed the same.

"I think you'll be stuck with me for the next thirty-ish weeks. I'm going to make a final decision based on what we learn today. It's reassuring to know I'm in the care of someone who recognizes all options."

She nods again, makes another few notes on her tablet, then turns to me. "All right then. I'm going to head out to give you some privacy to change. When I get back, we'll do the exam, and I'll take some measurements to see if we can narrow down an estimated due date."

I can't help the laugh that escapes. "Oh, I can tell you the date, or at least the twelve hours of conception. There's only one option."

Dr. Barber smiles kindly. "That does make the math a bit

easier. But we'll still check on things and make sure you have a picture or two to head home with. Here's a gown to change into, and I'll be sure to grab some clean instruments from next door." With a wink, she pushes back in her chair and shuts the door softly behind her.

I take a deep breath and after hiding my underwear—seriously, why do we do that?—I hop up on the exam table.

"You got this, Michelle." I hype myself up and stare at a spot on the ceiling while focusing on my breath. In and out.

There's a knock on the door before Dr. Barber sticks her head in. After seeing I'm ready, she slides through the opening of the door and another young woman in rose scrubs follows.

"This is Sabrina," the doctor says. Sabrina waves and smiles a kind smile before rolling over a machine. When she reaches the exam table, she says, "We'll talk you through what's happening. First, we're going to prep the wand with a sleeve and some lube."

I eye the wand warily before looking back at my caretakers. "Well, it all seems pretty familiar so far. Condom, lube when needed, long thing headed for my vagina. What's next?"

They both chuckle at my humor, though their eyes hold a look telling me they know I'm deflecting. "This might seem pretty familiar then, too." Dr. Barber says before pulling out the stirrups. "If you want to slide down for me and get situated, we'll get started."

My heels nestle into the metal foot holds. I find that spot on the ceiling again, preparing myself as they warn I might feel some pressure. There are a few moments where it's very clear I'm being probed with something medical before I hear it.

Ba-dum, ba-dum.

My eyes lock on the screen, the black and white static taking the shape of a blob, pulsing in time with the rhythm I hear through the speaker. "Well, that's definitely something new."

Dr. Barber squeezes my calf as she continues to move the wand, getting all the angles and measurements they need. I hear Sabrina click a few keys on the keyboard. "I'll go grab those copies for you to take home." She hands me a towel as she hangs up the wand and rolls the cart away before she squeezes out the door.

My head falls back on the pillow again. All those questions, all my research, silenced by a heartbeat and a grainy blob. There will be a time and place for them, but for now, I can't break myself out of this moment.

"You can sit up whenever you're ready, Michelle. Everything looks healthy and viable. I'll be sure Sabrina brings you some pamphlets on all of your options. Do you want her to bring those pictures too?"

I nod. "Yes. I'll take all the information you have, but I want those pictures too, please." My eyes fill with tears, my chest tightening, the loose gown suddenly constricting. It's only me. This decision is all on me.

"Will do. Look over those pamphlets and don't hesitate to ask if you have any more questions." Honestly, Dr. Barber should give classes on bedside manner. I know later I'll reflect on how her tone is perfect—gentle, calm, non-judgmental, but sure.

I shake my head no, still unable to formulate any questions, and hear her get up and head for the door.

"Wait," I say, and her movements stop. "Do you . . . do you mind getting my friend, Jax, from the waiting room? Maybe she can bring the stuff back in with Sabrina? She's probably the only Jax out there, but brown hair, bangs, blue eyes so big they'd look at home on Bambi?"

"Sure thing. They'll be right with you. One of those pamphlets has the recommended appointment schedule listed in it. You can make an appointment on your way out or call us later. Up to you."

"Thank you, Dr. Barber, for everything."

The door closes softly behind her. The ceiling starts to swirl in front of my eyes. A tear trickles down my cheek. I know I should sit up, get dressed. Twenty minutes ago, I worried about being late for work? Such a minor thing to fret over when I keep hearing the steady thump of a heartbeat in my ears.

The door creaks open again, and Jax comes into my line of sight.

"Hey, there. Everything okay?"

"Well, I'm pregnant. There's a baby in there and everything." Her hand finds mine and I squeeze tight.

"Good to know six pregnancy tests is a number to be trusted."

"I lied. It was actually twelve." I laugh at myself before wiping my eyes and sitting up.

Jax waves a stack of papers in her hands. "A nurse who looks suspiciously like Zoë Kravitz handed me all of this for you."

I groan. "I knew she looked familiar. How could I miss a doppelgänger for number three on your hall pass list? Preston will never forgive me."

"It'll be our little secret." She points at the two smaller pieces of paper face down on the top of the pile. "Are these . . ." She trails off, her voice lifting into a question.

"Yup. Those are photos of the little cumulus cloud shaped thing in my uterus."

Jax snorts. "You would."

I shrug. "At least I'm consistent. Flip it over. I need you to bear witness to the moment."

Jax turns the photo over and gasps, covering her mouth with her hand. "Holy shit. There really is a cumulus cloud baby inside you, isn't there?" I see her eyes start to water before she blinks the moisture away and locks eyes with me.

"How are you? Too big of a question? Tell me if I need to come up with a different one instead."

I laugh. "For right now, I'm okay. When I was lying there, I had a moment of feeling really alone. And I know if I decide to go through with this pregnancy, there will be a lot of moments of being alone, but—"

"I'm glad you decided to not make this one of them. I'm here for you. Whatever you need, whatever you decide to do."

My eyes start to water again. Ten weeks and no tears, but ten minutes of doctor confirmed pregnancy, and it's waterworks city. "I know you are. Thank you. For now, I need to get changed and get to work. There will be many more lists in my future, but I think I'll let it all simmer."

She lifts up the stack of papers, pamphlets, and photos and indicates her head to the door. "I'll wait for you right out there."

A few minutes later, I find Jax right where she said she'd be. We walk down the hallway and she slows as we pass the desk with one of the receptionists behind it.

"Do you need . . ." she trails off.

I follow my gut. "Yeah, I think I will make an appointment. I can always cancel it if I need to." She squeezes my arm again as I step up to the counter, smile, and schedule for four weeks from today. I look over my shoulder as she says the date and time and smile, seeing Jax typing into her phone. I'd bet the rights to choosing my on-air outfits for the next month she's putting this appointment in her calendar, too. We may not have known each other long, but I know I've got a good one in her. I need to tell Laurel, too. I'll need all the cheerleaders I can get.

We exit the front door, blinking at the bright sunlight, jarring after so much time inside.

"Well, I'm going to grab the bus this way," I say, pointing over my shoulder with my thumb.

"I'm going to go write in a new coffee shop I found while I was in the waiting room that way," Jax says, pointing in the opposite direction. "Text me tonight. Let me know how you are?"

I nod, and we hug before she starts walking away.

"Hey, Jax!" I yell after her, and she whirls around immediately.

"No reading any of your books until they're at least thirteen, okay?" I put my hand on my stomach.

Her face breaks into a wide grin as she laughs at me. "Guess I better find myself some new books to gift then."

We wave and carry on our ways. As I sit on the bus, I click on my list making app. After a second, I force myself to close it and open up the latest forecast projections from NOAA instead. I meant it when I told Jax I need to let it simmer. I look at the data and sink into the familiarity of analysis mode, pushing everything else to the back burner. Nothing like a potential string of strong storms to shove all thoughts to the background. Little Cumulus will still be there waiting for me after I warn everyone with Nats tickets for tonight they may see more tarp than turf out on the field.

CHAPTER
Six

HUNTER

Ten weeks pregnant

If I close my eyes and feel the rhythm of the boat as it crests the small waves, I can almost imagine the wide-open ocean around me. While I didn't share Preston's hyper fixation with marine animals growing up, I do feel sense of peace on the water.

"No, Senator Marsden specifically requested—"

"I don't give a fuck if the ghost of Ronald Reagan himself appears in that office, you need to stay until—"

I groan quietly as I lift my head from where it rested on the side of the boat and blink behind my sunglasses. Nothing like a boat ride with your two workaholic brothers to ground you in reality. Not an open ocean, but the brown and muddy Potomac. The sunshine and cool breeze of the unofficial start to summer persists and I tip my head again, enjoying the rays on my face. I've been picking up whatever shifts I can in local restaurant kitchens around Holly Ridge at all hours of the day and night while I wait for something permanent to open up. It's nice to sit and relax.

"Fucking interns," Duncan and Preston say in unison, lowering their phones at the same time. We all laugh. People can usually pinpoint us as brothers when we're all together, but sometimes things happen that leave no doubt.

"You know, Duncan, if you're not careful, people will get confused," I say, arranging my face in what I hope portrays a picture of innocence. "Are you saying fucking interns, like a descriptive? Or do you mean it more as an action—"

"Fuck off," he replies, flipping me the bird as Preston chuckles. "I have never slept with an intern, and you know it."

"I know, I know. Sorry, big bro. The opportunity lay before me." We all lapse into a comfortable silence, sipping from our beers as the guy Duncan hired to drive the boat turns us around at the northern end of the city, and we head back south.

"So, what did Hayden give you to get him out of this little joy ride?" I ask. It's time to get to the bottom of why Duncan insisted we take this boat out in the first place.

"Since he and Charlotte are hosting on their rooftop, he promised he'd do an extra three months of philanthropy committee if he could stay behind. Plus, Spencer ordered something from Wegmans to contribute since he can't be here. It's delayed, so they need to go pick it up, too."

"You know," Preston says, running his hand through his brown hair, the strands lighter than Duncan's, but darker than my dirty blond. "I'm starting to think Hayden actually enjoys philanthropy duty, and he's not actually bothered by you assigning it to him."

Preston, as usual, figured out the truth. Duncan's face goes pensive. To distract him before he gives it too much thought, I blurt out what I've been thinking. "So, this thing you wanted to talk to me about. You know, the big secret I had to travel to DC for and all."

"Yes, right." Duncan sets down his beer and straightens up. If he were wearing a suit instead of a polo and board shorts, I think he'd straighten the tie and button the jacket. "I wanted to talk to you about your meal planning business."

I shoot a look at Preston, who has the decency to look a little guilty.

"It's a good idea, Hunt. Listen to him."

"Okay, Judas," I say. My eyes focus on Duncan, but my ears are full of white noise and my stomach is twisting. Coming to Duncan for funding for my business idea has always been something I've known is an option. But I hoped to find another way. I intentionally didn't mention to Duncan how much it's grown for this very reason.

"Hunter, are you listening to me?"

I shake my head and my ears clear. "Sorry. Having a slight existential crisis. Can you repeat yourself?"

He smiles the smile he's worn since our mom died and he took it upon himself to become another parent, whether we wanted him to be or not. I can hear what he's not saying out loud: At least it's an internal crisis Hunter's having this time. Hindsight being what it is. I know I didn't make things easy on him, or my dad, or anyone really, while growing up, but I'm really trying now.

"I'd love to give you a graduation gift. Some start-up money to allow you some time and space to see how this thing can grow. I know you're killing yourself with all those shifts wherever you can find them. This will allow you to find the right job in the right kitchen and still make a living."

I set my beer down and lean forward, my forearms on my knees and level him with a look of my own. "Would you make this offer to anyone else?"

Duncan looks surprised. "What do you mean? Of course I would. Hayden has a start-up housed under my company."

"Sure," I nod. "But he came to you with a business plan, right? Plus, he has real-world business experience. And you're getting a portion of his profits when he starts to make them."

"Well, sure, but—"

I hold up my hand. "I appreciate what you're trying to do, Dunc, I really do. I know you have my back. And I know you're framing it as a gift, but if"—I raise my voice to stop him from interrupting—"I do ever decide to broaden this idea into something bigger, I'll come to you with a business plan, a proposal for returns for you, benchmarks, targets, the whole nine yards."

Duncan reclines with a gleam in his eye looking a lot like respect. "All right then. I appreciate that."

"So instead"—I take a sip of beer to up the tension—"you can gift me something normal. You know, like a car." I wink to let him know I'm joking, or else he probably would have one delivered before I get home.

He lifts his beer. "Am I allowed to propose a toast?"

"Has anyone ever successfully stopped you when you tried?" I volley back.

"Nope," he says, a smug tilt to his mouth. "To new beginnings and great achievements. I'm proud of you, Hunt." Preston clinks his beer with ours, mouthing, "sorry," to me before we all tip the bottles to drain them.

"Now then," Duncan says, looking at his watch. "Right on schedule to be getting back to the wharf and up to the rooftop. Try to be a bit more gracious when Hayden and Charlotte surprise you with the cake Spencer ordered than you were with as my gesture, okay? They don't have my thick skin."

My cheeks warm from more than the sun. I'm so used to being the problem, somewhere along the way I got really bad at taking recognition for what I've accomplished. It may be time to work on that.

Preston and Duncan complain about the humidity in DC, but tonight, there's none of that pesky stuff to be found. This part of the rooftop of Charlotte and Hayden's building looks out over a stretch of highway I can't remember the number for. It's different than I'm used to after small-town New England life. But we're facing west, and the sun sets here like it does everywhere else, inching toward the horizon.

I look around at a mix of people whose names I'm positive I won't remember. Friends from various parts of my brothers' lives are here. Duncan is manning the grill, surprising everyone by putting on the apron his assistant brought when she showed up.

Preston walks up to me, a beer in each hand. He thrusts one at me. "So, you overwhelmed yet?"

I laugh and take a swallow, enjoying the cold liquid as it slides down my throat. "It's a lot of faces and names to take in. But you all have built something here. A community. Nice to see."

Preston nods as he takes his own look around, his bottle tilted to his lips. "It is nice. It'll be hard to leave next year to move back to Massachusetts. My apartment will be open though, you know. If you wanted to come join in all this." He gestures to the people laughing and talking, someone from Preston and Jax's office playing beer pong alongside someone I'm pretty sure works with Charlotte.

"Why, so you can keep a few hundred miles between us? Switch spots?"

He smacks me lightly on the arm. "No, jackass. But if you're looking for people to be around and lift you up, you've got it here. We worry about you up there by yourself."

"I'm not by myself." Preston levels me with a look. "Okay, sure Dad and Margaret aren't necessarily in my social circle, but really, I'm okay." He looks like he doesn't believe me, which makes sense when I'm not sure I believe myself. Distraction time.

"Anyway, aren't you going to be up there alone? Or will a certain bang-having author be accompanying you on your next adventure?"

Preston's cheeks darken to match the streaks of pink starting to form in the sky as the sun sinks lower. "It's a possible consideration. She says she can write from anywhere she has a desk, a coffee pot, and a cat. She's joking about the cat. I think . . ."

I laugh, not at all sure she *is* joking. That'll be fun to watch. "Where is Jax, anyway?"

Preston pulls out his phone to check the time. "She should be here any minute. Her friend Michelle had an appointment she wanted Jax to go to with her, but they're on their way."

As if he summoned her with his words, the brunette in question appears, waving our way from across the rooftop. Behind her, a flash of auburn disappears around the corner. Maybe it's the way the golden hour light caught the strands, but it looks so much like the color of Clyde's hair. I see her auburn locks in my dreams, so it makes sense I think I'm seeing it everywhere in DC. A whole family with her hair color passed me in the airport yesterday, but none wore it as well as she does.

Not for the first time this weekend, I take out my phone, tilting the screen so no one can see what I'm looking at. I downloaded Tinder again on the plane ride down here. Our chat exists, but Clyde's message thread now reads from "Unknown User" instead of WeatherGirl85. She must have deleted her account. I'm not sure why I expect her to have a sixth sense I'm in the city again and reactivate her account, but I can't help checking every chance I get.

A generic greyed out head icon awaits me. My stomach dips with disappointment—again.

"You okay over here, man? Looks like Jax got held up, so I'm going to go save her."

I wave him off, taking advantage of the time alone to sit in a chair facing the outer wall of the roof and open the gig app I use to book new clients for my meal planning business. If you told me two years ago I would be checking on work, at a party, on a long weekend, I'd say you have the wrong twin. But the rush of answering the questions and inquiries waiting for me is something I hope never gets old. My mind wanders to Duncan's offer while I add a few things to my project management app, so I can dive in on my trip home on Monday.

Finally, I tuck my phone away before anyone can accuse me of Duncan-like work habits at a social gathering. I finish the last of my now too-warm beer and look around for the recycling. My eyes travel over the crowd, skipping past the corner next to the elevators before my gaze is yanked back. Standing next to Jax is Clyde. My WeatherGirl. I'd think I'm imagining her if not for the look of absolute shock on her face. I'm frozen in place. I've dreamed about this moment, but now that it's here, I have no idea what to do.

I look to Jax next, and her matching look of shock is what finally propels me into motion. I weave through furniture at a pace faster than polite for a rooftop gathering, but I can't imagine letting her get away again. Clyde's eyes open wide when she realizes I'm headed straight for them and yanks Jax around the corner.

When I turn the corner myself, I see there's a single-person bathroom there, the occupancy tag turned to red for "In Use." I prop myself against the wall. With us being on the roof, fifteen stories above ground level, I'm fairly confident there isn't a window in there for them to sneak out of. But I watched too many *Friends* re-runs with Margaret in my life to be one hundred percent sure.

No, I'll wait right here. They have to come out sometime. I scrub my face with my hands, trying to activate my brain. What does someone say to the one-night stand they haven't stopped thinking about when they run into them by chance at a Memorial Day picnic. I'm not sure even Hallmark would have a card for this.

CHAPTER
Seven

MICHELLE

Ten weeks pregnant

"Ugh," I say, watching the numbers tick up as the elevator climbs. "I always thought women were exaggerating when they said they always have to pee when pregnant. Lesson learned, it's true! Decades of women aren't lying to us . . . about this."

Jax tries and fails to hold in a giggle. "I mean, you also drank about a liter of water on the ride over here."

"Well, pregnancy is full of contradictions! Stay hydrated, but even if you don't, you'll still pee all the time." I try to send her a stern look while I talk, but end up giggling, too.

"Ugh, okay, one more trip to the bathroom, and hopefully, I'll be able to pretend to not be pregnant for a while. Remind me, does Preston know we were on baby business?"

"Yes, but I told him if anyone asks to say you had an appointment and needed a second set of ears. All that time in politics has made him good at being vague."

The doors of the elevator slide open, and we walk out of the vestibule onto the rooftop, a soft breeze whispering through my hair. "See, my mother would say what he's actually good at is lying, and he doesn't need politics to do that. He's born with it by being a man."

Jax reaches down to squeeze my hand. "That might be an anecdote for your therapist, not for a party." Her words have a teasing lilt to them, and I know if I actually needed to talk about the way pregnancy is twisting up feelings about my mom, she'll listen. She already has, more times than she should need to, in the last few weeks. My therapist found a slot for me to bump up to weekly sessions starting this week, so I'll have another outlet soon.

"A good note. This is why you're the writer, and I read off a teleprompter."

"I mean, you write those forecasts and then read them."

"And have them approved ahead of time by an old white man," I grumble. "Okay, see, there I go again. I'm going to the bathroom now and when I come out, I will be a less grumpy, more charming Michelle."

Jax points around the corner. "My bathroom sense is tingling and saying it's around that corner there."

"I'm so glad you use your powers for good and not evil." Jax lives with irritable bowel syndrome and has developed an uncanny knack for finding a bathroom in a place she's never been before.

"Toilets might say otherwise," she says with a wink before shooing me. "Didn't you really have to pee?"

The urge comes back, stronger than before, and I speed walk my way around the corner, saying a quick thanks when I find it unoccupied. I take a quick moment of peace to check my email. Ignore the one from my boss. Star the follow up from the baby proofing consult Jax and I did this afternoon, gifted by Laurel and Caitlin frighteningly fast after I told them the news. Apparently, Caitlin "knew someone." I swipe through more junk, before an email from Tinder pauses my thumb.

Subject Line: Lonely Long Weekend? It doesn't have to be. Reactivate today. A huff of a laugh escapes before I swipe it into trash too. It'll be a good long time before I'm ready to swipe on profiles instead of emails. Maybe eighteen years plus thirty weeks.

After I wash my hands, I tug on my dress. My body doesn't look much different yet. I've gotten questions if I was pregnant long before the two lines on the backup tests appeared. People don't know how to handle themselves when women's bodies don't conform to "normal" standards. I know I can't hide being pregnant forever. But along the same lines of people not keeping their opinions about my body to themselves, I know intrusive inappropriate questions will be lobbed my way on the regular once people find out. I'm not ready.

I swing the door open and jump to find Jax leaning against the wall. "You jinxed me," she teases. "Preston's right around the corner talking to Hayden and Hayden's girlfriend, Charlotte. He'll protect you until I'm done." With that, she locks herself in the bathroom.

Sometimes, it's easy to forget Jax and I have only known each other for ten weeks. A personal crisis each can do that for a friendship. But it also means I don't know all of her people yet. She promised she wouldn't abandon me when I tried to beg off coming tonight, making a case I can't hide away for the next thirty weeks.

I spot Preston, as promised, by the snack table. My eyes scan the rest of the crowd while I walk, seeing if there's anyone else I know when I hear it. A laugh I last heard right next to my ear, from the pillow beside me. My head whips toward the sound, and I stop dead when I see the man Preston's talking to. He looks exactly like . . . I shake my head and blink my eyes a few times. A man by the grill yells "Hayden," and the guy who looks just like my Bonnie, RidgeMan93, lifts his beer in acknowledgment. The arm he raises is bare of both sleeves and tattoos, and my heart sinks when I realize it can't be him.

Preston spots me and comes over to give me a hug. "While it's the two of us, how did the appointment go?"

I force myself to focus on the man in front of me instead of staring at the one-night stand lookalike apparently named Hayden. "It was great. Really helpful. They reassured me the second room is plenty big enough for everything the baby needs for at least a few years. In my rational mind, I knew it would be, but it's helpful to hear from experts. They also . . ." I trail off as I take in Preston's face. The features seem more familiar now than they ever did before.

"Also?" He prompts me to continue.

"Also recommended everything I would need to make the place baby proof." I finish my train of thought. "All in all, really helpful."

"Well, that's great," Preston says. "I'm glad you can stay put. I know moving is stressful enough without everything else. At least it's not twins, huh?"

At the word "twins," my spine stiffens, remembering something Jax mentioned about the Brandt brothers. Preston confirms it an instant later.

"Luckily, Mom and Dad already had two kids' worth of stuff when Hayden and Hunter came along. Hey, you okay? You're pale all of a sudden. Do you need some water?"

"Sure, that would be great. Do you mind grabbing me some? I think I need to go to the bathroom again." Somehow, I manage to not sputter like my brain is exploding, which it absolutely is. Preston walks away, presumably to get me water, because he follows through like that. I race around the corner and find the "In Use" placard on the lock.

"Jax?" I call through the door.

"Be right out," she replies.

I rest my back against the wall. The door opens a few seconds later and Jax comes to stand in front of me.

"Shit, Michelle, are you okay? You look like a ghost."

I laugh, wincing at the slightly hysterical nature of the sound.

"You and Preston are really meant for each other. He'll be finding us with water in a second. But first, the day we met, we went to brunch and then that lingerie store. Was Hunter in town?"

Jax thinks for a moment, a confused look on her face. "Yeah, actually he was. He came to the river clean up earlier that day. Why?"

I laugh again, this one tinged with a little bit of a sob. "It's a really fucking small world, that's why. We better go out before Preston comes looking."

"Wait. Do you think . . . Hunter is the father?" she whisper yells, starting after me.

"I about had a heart attack when I heard Hayden's laugh out there. My heart definitely stopped when I saw the person the laugh belongs to. Then Preston reminded me Hayden has a twin. So, unless there's a third Brandt brother who looks exactly like them, I think there's a really good chance."

"Michelle," Jax whisper screams again as we round the corner. "Hunter is—"

I come to a dead stop when I catch sight of the tattooed, beautiful man who's been haunting my dreams and changed my life so irrevocably without knowing it. He's back lit by the sunset, but there's still enough light for me to know he sees me too.

"Here," Jax finishes, coming to a dead stop next to me. "Is that him? Your one-night stand?" she mutters out of the side of her mouth?

I swallow. "Yup."

Clyde, real name Hunter, makes his way across the roof toward us, moving like I might be a mirage in danger of disappearing if he can't get to me fast enough. I panic and yank Jax's arm, moving us back toward the bathroom.

"You know, there are parties I spend all night in the bathroom for, but this is really different," she jokes, staring at the door I lock behind us. I'm starting to have trouble catching my breath, hearing myself wheeze. Jax jumps into action, grabbing one of the sanitary napkin bags next to the toilet. "Here, breathe into this. It's going to be okay."

I breathe in and out for a few beats until finally my breathing returns to normal. My eyes close and I slump against the wall.

"He's a good guy, Mich. They all are."

A tear trickles down my cheek as I roll my head to meet her gaze. "I'm not sure even *good guy* prepares you for, 'Hi, it's Hunter, isn't it? I'm Michelle, and by the way, I'm carrying our baby.'"

"It's a lot. I won't pretend it isn't. But there's a first time for everything. I think the Brandts could manage to surprise your mom."

That gets a snort laugh out of me. "I don't think that's possible. And fuck, he's younger than Preston, right? He is. Preston said there were already two sons when the twins were born. Preston's younger than me, which means . . ."

"One thing at a time. Keep breathing. The first thing is we have to open that door, and you have to say something to him. Why don't you start with hi? Because with the look on his face when he saw you, he's not going anywhere without talking to you."

I groan. "Why isn't there a window in this thing we can crawl out of?"

"Because you're not Rachel Green. This is real life, and we're hundreds of feet in the air."

"You and your logic. Okay." I walk to the sink and dab under my eyes with a paper towel and run my fingers through my hair. "Let's do this."

Deep breath in, deep breath out, and I open the door. Hunter's there, leaning against the wall, one foot propped against the brick. My eyes go immediately to his arms, eyes tracking from his wrists where he's stuck his hands into his pockets, up to the colored ink as it disappears underneath his shirt sleeve.

When I can't put it off any longer, I look to his face and find his eyes waiting for mine. He pushes off the wall and moves to me.

"I'm . . . going to go find Preston about some water," Jax says, peeling off and leaving us alone. When she's safely behind Hunter, she pauses to give me a wink and a double thumbs up before disappearing around the corner.

We stand in silence until I think I might scream.

"So, you're a Brandt," I say, at the same time his says, "I can't believe you're here." Guess the quiet bothered him too.

"Wait, you know my last name? That's a stupid question. You know my brother's fiancée or . . . well . . ."

"Whatever they are now," I finish, a soft smile breaking through despite my nerves. "So yes, I do. And your first name too. Hunter. Hi."

"Hi. You know, this seems unfair. You don't have to call me Bonnie anymore, but—"

"Michelle. Lewis. I'm Michelle Lewis," I say in a rush. It suddenly feels so wrong to live in a world where this man doesn't know my real name.

"Michelle. It suits you." He pulls a face. "I'm not sure why I said that. What the fuck does that even mean?" He laughs nervously.

"Well, what came first for you, the name or the fascination with deer?" I nod toward the solid black four-legged animals with horns standing in front of shaded trees blended into the designs on his left arm.

He looks down. "This was one of the first parts of this arm's sleeve. A reminder to balance the instincts of the hunter with the innocence of the hunted." He meets my eyes again, the glacial blue clear with honesty. So much for a joke to break the ice.

I take a step back, wondering how there can be so little air when we are standing in the open evening. The sky shifts into twilight. Hunter takes a step forward.

"How are you here right now?" he asks.

"Well, I'm here in DC because I got a job I couldn't turn down I now hope I don't grow to hate." He shakes his head with a chuckle as he takes another step toward me and my back meets the bathroom door. At least he still finds me a little bit funny. "But I'm here tonight because my cousin Laurel works with Preston and Jax."

He nods, stretching his hand out to brush his fingers through the hair above my shoulder. "Sorry, I should have asked if it's okay if I touch you. But I . . ." He takes a shuddery breath in. "I needed to know you were real."

My hand reaches up without a conscious instruction from my brain and cups his cheek. He leans into it, the warmth of his skin tingling up the length of my arm. "I know the feeling."

"Michelle, listen—"

"Hunter!" A call comes from the main rooftop area. It sounds like Hayden. Hunter swears and steps back before his twin appears around the corner. "Oh!" Hayden sounds surprised to find us both back here. "Uh, it's our turn for beer pong. You coming?"

Hunter looks at me, his eyes searching for something, before answering his brother. "I'll be there in a minute."

My heart plummets. Wanting to know I'm real and wanting to spend time with me are two different things. My mind searches for a way to get his number, imagining being able to call him with the news after he's back . . . wherever he lives.

"Look, I promised Hayden we'd play together. It's been years since we've had the chance. But I'd love to spend more time with you. But not here surrounded by a majority of my family. Can I see you tomorrow? We have a whole thing planned on Sunday and I fly home Monday, but I can get out of tomorrow."

I nod, my heart skipping in my chest when it shoots back up and lodges itself firmly in my throat instead. Tomorrow. If I want to tell him in person, I have to figure out how to do it—and find the nerve—in the next twenty-four hours. No biggie.

"Here. I'll put my number in your phone?" He says it like a question. I see doubt written on his face.

"Yes. Let's do that." I find my voice. "Give me yours, and I'll give you mine too."

We swap phones and type for the next few seconds. Our hands brush as we trade back, and my fingers tingle from the brief contact.

"I'll see you tomorrow then. Let me pick a place? I'd . . . I'd love to take you somewhere nice. Anything you don't eat?"

"Sushi and soft cheese," I say without thinking. Hunter's face stays mercifully blank, and I throw up a thanks none of the other brothers have procreated yet.

"Very specific. No sushi and no picnics. Got it."

"Hunter!" Hayden yells again, more impatient this time.

"I gotta go before he causes a scene. And to think he's the older twin." Hunter steps forward and wraps me in a brief hug, stepping back again before I can react. "Tomorrow," he says, making it sound like a promise as he backs away from me. I nod in response once more.

"Tomorrow," I say to myself, reeling from the last twenty minutes. Maybe Preston is on to something with that water thing.

I'm hit with the sudden urge to lie down and know it's time to leave. At this point, if I stay, I'll only end up staring at Hunter the rest of the night and making it weird.

I leave the little bathroom alcove for the last time and make my way to the elevator lobby. I hit the down button and look at the table sitting below the metal panel. Sitting on it is a bottle of water, resting on a napkin that says, "Michelle." My eyes start to water again and I look through the glass door. Jax is standing there smiling and makes the universal sign for call me before turning back to her group, not wanting to draw attention I'm leaving not all that long after we arrived.

The doors ding open, and I step on, unlocking my phone to call a ride share car to get home. I can't stomach the Metro right now. My phone screen lights up, displaying a new contact card. The name above the number reads Bonnie with a few mountain emojis and a deer emoji. A smile so big breaks across my face. I'm glad I'm alone so I'll never need to explain it. Whatever happens tomorrow, I can't help but be glad life brought us back to each other.

Epistolary Interlude #1

BRANDT BROTHERS GROUP CHAT

Hayden
You guys are never going to believe this.

> **Hunter**
> Seriously? You couldn't do this in the chat without me?

Hayden
Hunter got himself a DATE last night and is skipping out on poker night.

Duncan
You're just mad because his tells are the only ones you can read, so you're going to lose all your money.

Hayden
That's only seventy-five percent of the reason. He also won't tell me who she is. I know she's a redhead. Did anyone invite anyone with red hair?

Preston
Funnily enough, I did not categorize our invites by their hair color.

Spencer
You should have told Hayden you were sick and snuck out, Hunter. It worked for you in high school.

Hunter
Would have been easier. Silly me to think Hayden would understand me being away from him for a whole three hours. At least I'll be in a different part of the city and not in the next room.

Hayden
That's different. Charlotte wanted to congratulate me on our beer pong victory.

Spencer
Gross. You all really need to keep earplugs in the guest room supply basket.

Hunter
I ordered a 64-pack last night.

Duncan
Where are you taking her, Hunt? I have standing reservations at a few places. You can use one. I'm stuck at work until poker night.

Hunter
That's what started this whole thing. I asked Charlotte to weigh in on two places. Hayden heard me, and basically, you're caught up.

Hayden
I don't understand why you didn't just ask me.

Hunter
Because your favorite place to take Charlotte is District Taco.

Spencer
I mean, their food is really good, Hay, but that's not very fancy.

Hayden
We go other places. How did this end up turning on me?

Preston
Funny how that worked out, huh…

Spencer
Though I still want to know where you're going, Hunter.

Duncan
Hunt?

Hayden
He said to tell all of you he's going on do not disturb for the night, we're all assholes, and he loves us. Me most of all.

From: RBauer@KUSN.com
To: MLewis@KUSN.com
Subject: Proposal

Michelle,

Are you available to come into the station at 11:00 a.m. tomorrow? I have a proposal to run by you, and it has to be tomorrow. I think you'll find it very interesting.

I'll expect to see you then.

Ray

Jax
Have you decided what you're going to do about your boss's offer?

Laurel
I know it sounds tempting, but you already work too much. I'm worried about the strain on le bebe.

Michelle
I don't know that I can pass it up. He's offering me the chance to do what I want, why I took this job. And it's more money, which is a good thing. You know with Cumulus and all.

Laurel
I can't believe you're insisting on calling the baby that. No one's going to have any idea what you're talking about.

Michelle
And that's a bad thing? Besides, I'm leaving all the cute names for you and Caitlin. Y'all will pull that off much better than I.

Jax
How are you feeling about tonight? Where's he taking you?

Michelle
He said it's a surprise, but gave surprisingly detailed suggestions for the level of dressiness that's appropriate.

Laurel
Sounds like Charlotte to me.

Jax
Yeah, definitely. Sweet of him to think to ask though.

Laurel
Have you thought about how you'll break the news?

Michelle
I keep writing things down and then deleting them. I spent about twenty minutes in CVS seeing if maybe Hallmark had a card for this.

Jax
And?

Michelle
They definitely don't.

Laurel
Well, if the meteorologist thing doesn't work out, you have a great business idea?

Jax
Cards to break the awkward news in life.

Laurel
Cawks?

Michelle
Please say that out loud, L.

Laurel
Lol, whoops. You know they're not my thing.

Jax
Anywayyy we should let you go get ready for tonight. I'll get Preston to spill the beans on where you're going once he gets to poker night.

Michelle
You think they know?

Jax
I'm sure they know he has a date. Those brothers gossip more than a small-town nursing home. Whether or not they know it's you . . .

Laurel
Monica This Just Got Interesting.gif

Michelle
I think I might throw up. Is it normal to get morning sickness for the first time right before you tell the father?

Laurel
Yes

Jax
Yes

Michelle
Awesome.

Michelle
Call you tomorrow. 😘

CHAPTER
Eight

MICHELLE

Still ten weeks pregnant

I stand outside Code Red, a few blocks from my apartment. My lip won't have any skin left on it by the time Hunter gets here. Not that he's late. No, I'm ten minutes early, in case I caught traffic. You know, on the sidewalks.

Something pulls me to look to the left, and I spot Hunter walking up the street toward me. He's focused on the sidewalk in front of him and doesn't see me yet, so I enjoy the chance to take him in. His head bobs slightly, so I assume he's listening to music. He's wearing jeans that fit tight across his thighs. I make a mental note to check out his butt later. His tattoos are covered by a blazer, but the button-down shirt underneath boasts a colorful floral pattern that should make him look like he's headed for a Jimmy Buffet concert. Instead, it suits him. Hunter. The father of my child.

I'm back to chewing on my lip and look down at my midi sundress and wedge sandals. It's the same jade color as the lace bodysuit I wore that night. He seemed to like it then, and I figure it can't hurt anything now.

Suddenly a hand is on my face. I should startle, but his cedar scent is familiar right away. He pulls down on my chin to remove my lip from my mouth.

"I want to do that."

I burst out laughing. "Quoting Christian Grey? Is that how you think this evening is going to go?"

His grin could light up a mineshaft as he drops his hand. "I figured corny pick up lines are our thing. Inspiration struck." He looks me up and down. "You look beautiful."

My skin heats, and I once again curse my red hair and fair skin.

"Shall we?" he says, pointing at the door.

"Sounds great. I'm starving." I walk in through the door he holds for me. He gives his name at the hostess stand, and after a moment, she leads us to a booth in the back. She promises a waitress will be by with waters soon and leaves us to get settled.

"So, while I walked up from the Metro, I recognized a few things. Your apartment is close to here, isn't it?"

"Yeah," I say. "I wondered if that was part of the appeal to this place."

"No, I didn't realize. I'm glad you didn't have to go far, but I don't want you to think I picked it being presumptuous or anything. I didn't compare it to your address. The vibe seemed cool, and the red made me think of you. Plus, there's a prohibition vibe to this place too. Hayden says the cocktails are amazing. Once he stopped giving me a hard time about skipping poker night."

"You're skipping poker night? You didn't need to do that."

"Red, there's nowhere else I'd rather be."

Five minutes into the evening and I'm positive my cheeks will be sore from smiling more than I have in the past month. I stop looking at the food to look at their drinks menu. I scan for mocktails and am relieved to see a variety of options. Maybe I can order one and slip under the radar it doesn't have any alcohol in it.

The waitress comes by to take our orders. I open my eyes a little wider when I say my drink's name and, being a girl's girl, she gets the hint and doesn't confirm if I know it's spirit free. I see Hunter scanning the menu for my drink after he says his order, so go in for a distraction.

"So, *50 Shades of Grey*, huh?"

"What's your question?" he asks, leaning forward on the table. He took his jacket off when we sat down and revealed a set of rolled-up sleeves my eyes keep being drawn to.

"My question is . . . you've read them?"

He traces my gaze to his forearms and flexes them a bit. How does he . . .

"My stepmother is a big romance reader. I moved with my dad to her town after I graduated from high school. Only me and my youngest brother, Spencer, lived there full-time. He had school as an avenue to make friends. I didn't really try to make any connections there. I got one random job after another and spent a lot of time at home. It turns out there is only so much internet you can surf, so I started sneaking books off her bookshelf. Though, turns out, I'm not as sneaky as I thought. She started to leave ones she thought I'd like sitting at the front of the shelves."

I smile, resting my head in my hand. "That's really sweet." I pause for a second and decide to probe a little bit. We're going to get personal by the end of the night anyway. "You said you read with your stepmother?"

It's already a dark room, but I can see Hunter's eyes as they darken. "Yeah, Margaret. She's wonderful. No evil stepmother trope here. My mom died when I was eight. Dad worked hard to keep all five of us together and pay off the debt left behind. We all dealt with it differently. My way tended to be more . . . destructive."

"Is that when the tattoo habit started?"

He rubs his arm absentmindedly. "No, nothing like that. We lived in a different small town then, but everyone knew the Brandt brothers, especially the troublemaker Hunter. No tattoo artist within thirty miles would touch me while I was underage, and I didn't have a way to get farther. But I had plans, for sure. I don't have a record, but I think small-town life is also to thank for that."

I nod. "Grief can impact people in lots of different ways."

"What about your family?" he asks, picking up a piece of bread someone dropped off on the table while we were talking.

I suppose I should have seen this coming, since I probed into his. I take a breath in and say it fast. "My Dad skipped town when I was three. I haven't seen him since. My mom did a decent job of not bringing men into the house while I still lived there, but it was one deadbeat after another. If she happened to find a good one, she'd find some flaw and leave him for a change. I spent a lot of time at the neighbors, or when she felt I was old enough, home alone. It's not the healthiest relationship in my life."

"You're an only child?"

I nod. "As far as I know at least. I've always been scared to do one of those DNA test kits. Find my dad with some other family that could make him stay? They were young when they had me. Logically, I know neither of them was ready, but it left its mark." My arm goes across my stomach absentmindedly while I talk. I tell myself I'm not repeating the cycle. I'm over twenty years older than my mom was when she had me. I consider men with the opposite instincts of how my mom would look at them. No guarantee what Hunter will want, once I tell him, but he deserves to know.

The waitress passes by for the fourth time, and we finally put in our order. Hunter talks with her about the dishes for a few minutes, taking her recommendation for an appetizer and main course. I'm not the most adventurous eater on a good day and I wasn't exaggerating when I told Jax and Laurel earlier I thought my morning sickness was starting.

"So, is food your thing?" I ask, grabbing a piece of bread myself.

"I'd call it one of my things, yeah." His eyes look around and he clears his throat. "I, uh, actually just finished my associate's degree in culinary arts. They say it's never too late to go back to school."

I take a drink of the mocktail the waitress dropped off. I'm impressed by the smooth service they provide without interrupting. A great place for a date. Though, I don't expect to have many more of those anytime soon.

"That's great. And I heard that sarcasm there at the end. Not everyone knows what they want to do with their life at eighteen, or hell, even at twenty-eight!"

"Twenty-eight was about the age for me, actually. I moved out on my own after catching my dad and Margaret on the couch coming home at 2:00 a.m. one too many times." I snort laugh. "Hey, when you find love again after raising five sons, he can get it. But it's not something I need to see."

"That's fair. And probably healthy. But you were saying you moved out?"

"I did, and I realized very quickly how used to Margaret's cooking I was. She loves to cook, and always made too much, so she'd leave leftovers in the fridge for me to heat up after a shift, or as a midnight snack after the bars closed. Remember, small-town New England. You walk to and from the bars, when there aren't feet of snow on the ground."

I grew up in Middle America, where if you didn't have a car, you might not see another soul for a week. I understand the concept now, but couldn't imagine it before college.

"So I asked her for a few easy starter recipes. I mastered those and then started experimenting with little changes here and there. Making things my own. I tried harder and more complex recipes, and before I knew it, I was the one cooking for them. I passed an advertisement for the culinary program at the community college in the next town over just under two years ago, and here I am."

He takes a big swallow of his drink, his cheeks pink. It seems he's not used to talking about his accomplishments or celebrating his wins. Very interesting.

"So, I couldn't help but notice you said you moved out when you were twenty-eight."

He groans. "I hoped you wouldn't pick up on that. I know what you must think, me living at home. But it took a while to pull my head out of my ass. But here I am. Fully de-assed. There's something about you that makes me not want to hide those parts of me."

I take a big gulp of my drink, wishing it had something stronger when I think of what I'm hiding from him. The waitress arrives with our dinners. After making sure we have everything we need, she tells us to enjoy our food. I hope we can—we didn't ask which dish pairs best with life-altering news.

"Thank you for being honest." I pick up the thread. "But no, you didn't let me finish. I'm more am doing the math. If twenty-eight is only a few years ago for you, that confirms the ninety-three in your handle is because you were born in 1993?"

"That's right. And let me guess. The eighty-five in yours is because you were born in 1985?"

I nod with my mouth full of a bite of my salad.

"So, you're a few years older than me."

"I'm a third grader older than you, Hunter."

He takes a bite of his sandwich, looking thoughtful and somehow looking hot with juice running down his face. The glistening on his chin reminds me of the other time we were together and he got his chin wet.

I take another big gulp of my drink. Maybe it's best this doesn't have any alcohol in it, the way I'm chugging it.

"I've never really considered myself a cougar kinda guy, but then again, I've never met a woman like you before."

I roll my eyes at his line, and somehow, it seems the movement detaches my brain from my mouth.

"How about a MILF kinda guy? Are you one of those?"

Hunter slows his chewing and swallows. "I mean, I'm not saying it's never happened, but I don't go looking for them." He sets his sandwich down, looking confused.

It's not nice to play with your food before you change their life forever, Michelle.

"Hunter, I'm pregnant."

CHAPTER
Nine

HUNTER

Yes, still ten weeks pregnant

I've had nightmares of that sentence being spoken at various times over the umpteen years since I lost my virginity. This though, this doesn't feel like a nightmare. More like a confusing, underwater, slow-motion movie.

"You're pregnant," I repeat.

Michelle nods, chewing on her lip again. I still would like to do that for her, but this might not be the time. Hell, depending on her answer to my next question, there might never be a time again.

"And you're telling me because you want to let me know you're seeing the father?"

"Well, I am seeing the father. I'm seeing him right now."

I laugh and rub a hand down my face. "You've got jokes, don't you?"

She winces. "I'm sorry. I've had a bit more time to adjust to this than you have. A few weeks actually."

"A few weeks. So, forgive me. Since you're telling me, that has to mean . . ."

"It's yours. There's no one else it could be."

"Got it. Sorry to insinuate—"

She puts her hands on top of mine, which is the first time I realize they're shaking. Shit, I'm not handling this well.

"It's okay. We don't know each other very well. It's a reasonable question to ask. I'm happy to bring in character witnesses, or a paternity test when it's available. Whatever you'd like."

I turn my hand over to grasp hers. "I believe you. I believed you when you said in March you didn't do that kind of thing often. And I believe you tonight. But thank you for offering. It means a lot."

The waitress comes by with our check and some boxes. I say thank you and turn to Michelle, her eyebrows raised high like mine.

"Damn, they're good at reading vibes here. Do you think they get this a lot? Because I sure as shit can't eat any more," she says.

I look down at the sandwich, remembering the rich flavors as they exploded on my tongue, dulled now with the news changing my world view.

"I don't think I can either. Wait! Are you feeling okay? How have things been? Wait. How. How is a great question. Those condoms were brand new."

Michelle shrugged and laughed. "You have strong swimmers that won't be contained? I'm not sure. I wasn't on any other birth control at the time, but my period hadn't been regular in a couple of months with stress from the move and the new job. And I'm feeling okay. Today brought some new queasy moments, but I'm not sure if that's the nerves of telling you or if I'm starting to experience some morning sickness."

"Is it because I crumpled them into my pocket?" I mutter to myself, her words clicking and I want to smack myself for thinking only about me. "I'm really glad you've been feeling okay so far. Have you been to the doctor? I know absolutely nothing about babies and the female body once we get beyond, well, you know, how we ended up here."

"I looked it up. Even if used perfectly, condoms are only effective ninety-eight percent of the time. Too bad we didn't play the lottery, huh? And uh, you do know your way around a body," Michelle says, her cheeks turning red like she can't believe she said that out loud. Her lack of filter is actually adorable. I'm sure once the shock wears off, I'll forever appreciate I learned I'm going to be a dad by the future mother of my child making a MILF joke. Mother of my child. Dad. Holy. Fuck.

I notice Michelle's hand isn't in mine anymore. She reaches for her purse on the booth seat next to her for something.

"No, no. I've got this. I asked you to meet up." I hurry and pull my credit card out of my wallet and set it in the folder with the receipt. Michelle brings her hands even with the top of the table with a white 3x5 piece of paper in her hand.

"I don't think this is going to pay the bill, though I'm happy to split it . . ." The waitress takes the folder off the table right as she says that causing us both to laugh.

"Like you said, they read the vibes." I wait for her to show me what's in her hand. I've seen enough movies and TV; I have a guess.

"Before I give you this, I should let you know. I'm planning on keeping the baby. I considered all my options, and that's the right path for me, assuming everything stays healthy. There are no expectations on you. I think I would have tried to track you down somehow in a few more weeks anyway, but there you were last night. And, no matter what comes next, I'm . . . I'm glad you were on that rooftop."

I really wish her hands were somewhere I could grab them. How hard it's been for her to face this all on her own over the past few weeks radiates off her in waves. To think, we were both thinking of each other, however far apart, neither of us knowing we are connected, not only by this baby, but by our family and friends.

"Thank you for telling me. It's, of course, your choice, and I'll support you all the way. I'd love to be involved." I stop there. My brain is spinning in the background, but I don't want to lose myself in that yet. Stay here, now. I don't want to miss this.

"Thank you. Anyway, I wasn't sure if you'd want . . . I mean, here. It's a sonogram photo from the last appointment. Baby is healthy. They gave me two copies. I wasn't quite sure what to do with the second one. I guess it's usually for the other parent. And now I've found the other parent. So, here." She stops her rambling and thrusts the picture into my hand.

My eyes start to water as I look down at a pixelated blob. "It looks like a cloud from SNES Super Mario World," I say, not able to take my eyes off the picture.

"I said the same thing. Well, I think it looks like a real cloud, you know, in the sky. But I keep calling them Cumulus."

"Cumulus?" I ask, meeting her eyes, unsurprised to find them a little wet too.

She nods. "That's the cloud type they look like. Occupational hazard."

I realize I never got a chance to ask her what she does. It sounds like something with the weather, but I want to know more. I want to know everything.

"I'm going to go to the ladies' room," Michelle says, and I nod. My eyes drift down to the picture in my hand. That's part of me. I made this thing. And I'm going to be sure I'm someone they can be proud of.

Michelle comes back to the table but doesn't sit down. "I think I need to go home. I built up a lot of adrenaline today and I'm crashing hard."

I jump out of the seat and wrap the blazer I borrowed from Hayden around her shoulders. Keeping up with their reputation, the waitress brings my card by right on cue. I pull three twenties out of my wallet and drop them on the table, thanking her for everything as I grab our boxes and steer Michelle out of the restaurant.

"Well, I'm this way," she says once we are out on the sidewalk.

"Michelle—I mean this in the kindest way—but you are off your rocker if you think I'm not walking you home."

"Oh. Okay," she says, and she turns and starts walking. I follow alongside her, keeping my hands to myself. How do we act around each other now? Earlier today my thoughts consisted of sinking between her thighs with her feet on my shoulders. Now, well, I still want to do that, but I also want to rub her feet. Go out at two in the morning and get whatever weird thing she's craving. I want to be a part of this. I just need to figure out how to get her to allow me in.

"Well, this is me," Michelle says, and I realize we've walked three blocks without saying a word.

"Shit. I'm sorry, my head is all over the place . . ."

"I understand. It's a lot to take in. Like I said, I don't expect you to do any—"

I grab her arms, wanting to stop the sensation of her slipping through my fingers. I loosen my grip immediately, so she knows she can step away if she wants, but damn, it's good to touch her.

"I want to be a part of this. With you. Let me . . ." The final piece clicks into place. "Do you have to work on Monday?"

"I don't have to do a forecast, no, but there's a thing I might need to go in for in the afternoon."

"Perfect. Can I take you to breakfast? Or better yet, can I bring groceries and cook you breakfast? There are a few things I need to work through." Her expression falls, small enough I wouldn't catch it if I'm not taking in every millimeter of her face. "Not about being a part of this. I'm one hundred percent sure. It's . . . other things . . . I don't want to get ahead of myself. But breakfast? Monday?"

"I have been dreaming of that scramble you made me . . ."

"Perfect. Then that's what we'll do. I'll text you, but let's say nine o'clock?"

Michelle nods. "Yeah. That works."

"I'll see you then. I'll wait out here until you get inside. Let me know when you're in your apartment with the door locked?" Michelle's vibes are trending toward spooked-cat-ready-to-flee. I want to be sure she lets me in on Monday.

She nods again. We may have only spent hours together, but I already know nodding covers for when she's too overwhelmed to speak. I wonder how to show her she can always speak her mind with me.

She walks up the few stairs to the outer door. Right as she steps through, ready to let the door close behind her, I lob my final shot, designed to get her out of her own head.

"Oh, and Michelle? I really hope that's not the only thing about me you've been dreaming of."

I think I hear a gasp, but she doesn't turn around to let me see her face. Still, a smile creeps onto mine while I wait for my phone to buzz, letting me know she is safely inside.

Her text arrives seconds later. I drop a pin, so I don't need to ask her for her address and open an app to request a ride share to Hayden's place. I hope I'll beat Hayden and Charlotte home. I need his help.

I spend the ride to Navy Yard making lists and writing down rambling thoughts. Trying to make sense of the jumble in my head. I manage to get back to the apartment first. On the couch with a glass of whiskey is where Charlotte and Hayden find me when they get home twenty minutes later.

"Hey Hunter, how was your night? We weren't sure if you'd be home tonight or not." Charlotte comes to sit on the couch next to me, smiling expectantly.

I paste on a fake smile. "Now, Charlotte. You know a

gentleman doesn't kiss and tell." I love Charlotte. She's perfect for my brother, and once I bring her into the know, she'll be so helpful and supportive. But this is something I need to talk through with Hayden first.

"Hey, Char, why don't you go ahead to bed? I'll be there in a little bit," Hayden says. Duncan teases him about only knowing my tells, but that's because we have the same ones.

"Got it. Twin thing." Charlotte stands up. "Night, guys." She reaches up to lay a peck on Hayden's lips and ruffles my hair as she walks past. He watches her walk down the hallway with a small smile before sitting in the seat she vacated.

"Do I need one of those?" He nods toward the glass of whiskey in my hand.

"Way ahead of you, bro." I flip up the cushion between us, revealing a storage compartment where I stashed another glass and the bottle before I sat down.

"What? I didn't know the couch had storage!" Hayden exclaims, leaning over to lift up the cushion on his other side. I nudge him in the shoulder to take the drink I pour for him. "Annnnd I'll explore it another time. What's up?"

"So. My date tonight."

"Finally. It's been driving me up a wall I don't know anything about her."

I laugh, taking another sip of the whiskey. "It's Michelle."

Hayden connects the dots. "Preston's coworker's cousin?"

"That's the one."

"So, you hit it off last night?"

"There's a bit more to it than that. Remember when I came to visit in March? You may have never realized, but I didn't come home one night. I snuck in before you and Char got up."

"Wait, what? Where were you? I know we're grown, man, but you need to tell someone where you are." Hayden looks pissed. This won't help.

"Well, Preston knew." I put my arm up to block his hand. "I know, I know, but you were really drunk and excited to get back to your girlfriend. I wasn't going to cockblock, nor did I want to have to listen to it. So, I found an alternative."

"Okay, but what does that have to do with tonight?" I stare at him, blinking. "Oh, shit, you hooked up with Michelle back then? She moved here not long before, right?"

I nod. "Yeah. We didn't exchange names or anything and promised it would be a one night thing. But I haven't been able to get her out of my head since. So, when I saw her last night, I had to spend time with her again."

"I know you don't do many repeats, so this is a big deal. She must be special. Why the long face?"

"I'm going to need you to put your hand in front of your mouth, so if you get the urge to yell when I say the next part, you can bite on it and not scare the shit out of Charlotte, okay?"

"Okay . . ." he says warily making a fist and holding it in front of his mouth.

"Michelle is pregnant." Hayden gets out a quick yelp before biting down on his hand. "And to come full circle, yes. It's my baby. I'm going to be a dad."

Hayden starts to turn red.

"Hay, breathe. I didn't tell you to hold your breath!"

He starts gasping for air, flexing his fingers and rubbing where the indents from his teeth were.

"You're not shitting me. This isn't a joke?"

"With how much trouble some people have getting preg-nant? Pregnancy should never be a punchline," I say, thinking about stories I overheard from some of the women in my cooking classes.

"Okay, so what are you going to do?" Hayden swigs the rest of the whiskey. He goes to pour another glass, but I stop his hand.

"First, no more drinks tonight. Second, I need you to promise to keep this between us. Only until Monday. If Char-lotte gives you a problem when she finds out, let me know. I'll tell her I asked you to."

"Charlotte's the best. She'll understand without us having to explain. Besides, it's only twenty-four hours. So done and done. What else do you need?"

"Here's what I have in mind . . ."

The next day, we do the citywide scavenger hunt Margaret bought for us to do together this weekend. We create a shared album, and it seems like she and Dad spend all day waiting for the next update, commenting and teasing us as soon as we post a new photo. It's a fun day, regardless if Hayden and I are dragging from being up until 3:00 a.m. working on my plan.

Everyone's set to go their separate ways when I pull Duncan aside.

"Hey Dunc, I need to ask you something. Well, two things."

"Anything. What's up?"

"First, I need to change my plane ticket to the latest flight out tomorrow. I'll pay for the difference if you let me know how much it is."

He waves his hand. "No, you won't. I'll get my assistant on it. What's number two?"

"Can you bump whatever godforsaken thing you've scheduled at 6:00 a.m. on a Monday holiday so we can get coffee? Or we can meet at your office. Wherever you would go to hear a business pitch on a holiday."

Duncan smiles broadly and grabs my shoulder. "I know the perfect place. I'll text you the details."

"You will, not your assistant?" Maybe I shouldn't bite the hand I'm hoping will help me, but he is my big brother.

"I know how to send my brother some details, smartass. I look forward to seeing whatever you've put together."

I turn around to find Preston, Jax, Charlotte, and Hayden waiting for me. "I'm going to go stay at Jax's," Charlotte announces. "Prez has to catch a last-minute flight out to meet the senator at whatever parade he's participating in tomorrow, so I'll be out of your hair. Don't stay up too late with whatever you're plotting. Okay, boys?"

Hayden and I exchange glances, and I catch Preston and Jax doing the same out of the corner of my eye. I think back to Jax's reaction on the rooftop deck Friday night. It's very possible she and Preston may have been playing dumb all day. The one time Hayden keeps a secret, and half the players involved already know.

We say our goodbyes and the three of them head off toward Capitol Hill for Preston and Jax's place. "All right." Hayden claps me on the shoulder. "We're going to need coffee, we're going to need pizza, we're going to need Pepto, and we're going to need ice cream."

"You know, taking away a few of those things would remove the need for the third."

"Wow, man. Fatherhood's really changed you." We look at each other for a second before we both bust up laughing. I throw my arm around Hayden's shoulders and set off for the Metro to head to Navy Yard. For the first time in my life, I have faith things are going to go my way. Let's hope Michelle sees things the same way I do.

CHAPTER

Ten

MICHELLE

Yup, ten weeks pregnant one more time

What do you wear when your baby daddy is coming over at 9:00 a.m. to cook you breakfast on a holiday? Honestly, not only has Hallmark failed to prepare me for this entire situation, but Vogue has too.

I take stock of my reflection in the bathroom mirror. My long hair is thrown up into a messy bun. Hopefully it's enough to hide the fact I haven't showered since our date on Saturday. I spent yesterday alternating between working on my proposal for this afternoon's meeting with my boss and experiencing my most severe morning sickness yet. It seems to have subsided when I woke up this morning. The dark circles under my eyes didn't do me the same favor. My concealer is doing the heaviest lifting today.

My leggings and blouse are casual enough for this morning. Throwing a blazer on as I leave the house will transform it into day-off-turned-work-opportunity-meeting chic when I need to head to the station. Maybe I should pitch this column to *Vogue*. Or at least *Cosmo*. Start a college fund for little Cumulus.

A slightly hysterical giggle escapes before it's cut off by a knock at the door. With one more quick glance, I take a deep breath and roll my shoulders back. *You can do this, Lewis.*

Opening the door, I find Hunter leaning against the doorjamb on the hinge side, reusable bags in each hand. "Someone was leaving as I walked up, so I let myself in the building. Hope that's okay."

My breath catches, his words not really registering. I'm soaking in the way he combines the domestic of carrying groceries—and caring for the environment!—with the edge his tattoos project. Tattoos are visible on his forearms and biceps, the latter bulging where they're tucked into the tight sleeves of his T-shirt from the weight of his groceries. The pressure of my teeth biting into my lower lip breaks me out of my stupor.

"Oh, shit. Hi. Come in." I move out of the way to let him into my apartment.

Hunter chuckles. "Hi yourself." He walks past me and heads to the counter to set his bags down. His cedar scent reaches my nose and lingers in the room as I follow him, suddenly finding it very hot in here.

"I brought a little bit of everything," he says, unloading item after item onto the counter. "You mentioned some morning sickness, so wanted to be prepared for how you were this morning." He turns to face me. "How are you feeling? You look a little flushed. Should you sit down?"

The sight of him in my kitchen, remembering the scramble he made me just ten weeks ago . . . is doing things to me. I've read about how increased libido can kick in near the end of the first trimester, but . . .

"Michelle? Can I get you some water? You look like you should sit." Hunter's tone is laced with concern as he approaches me. I hold up my hand as he reaches for my arm, not entirely sure I can be held responsible if he touches me.

"Just reliving some memories." More heat floods my face. Apparently, along with increased horniness, pregnancy is giving me an increased loss of filter. Hunter's face takes on a wicked smirk. Or on second thought, maybe it's him.

"Ah. Well, I could always help you sit on the counter too," he says, his voice teasing now he knows I'm not in mortal peril. His gaze follows mine to the part of the counter where he pressed between my legs and . . .

"So, what do we have for breakfast?" I say, clapping my hands and walking to the counter to break the spell. I know I'm talking too loudly, but Hunter goes with it, joining me.

"I prepped a few things at Hayden's last night. Like I said, I wanted to have options depending on how you were feeling. And I figured whatever we didn't use now, you could use later this week."

A warmth spreads from the center of my chest, completely unrelated to my lady parts this time. How long has it been since anyone has done anything to take care of *me*? Hunter looks at me expectantly as he explains the different options, his face light and enthusiastic. Okay, maybe his caretaking is doing a little *something* to my bits, but that's a bonus.

"All of that sounds delicious," I say, not entirely sure I could repeat anything he listed if he tested me. "Yesterday was a little rough in the sickness department, but this morning is better. Maybe nothing too heavy or greasy?"

"The frittata, basically a fancy scramble, yogurt, and fruit salad it is." He heads to my cupboards and seems to find the dish he's looking for on the first try. He continues his preparation while I stand there, entranced.

"So, other than the sickness yesterday, how's the rest of your weekend been?"

"Uh, it's been okay. I worked for most of the day yesterday anyway, so I kept close to the toilet."

"Is that something you do a lot? Work on weekends?" He

opens the oven door as he asks, frittata plate in hand, and stops short. "Uh, you don't cook much do you?"

I look in the oven to see the pots and pans I shoved in there while I unpacked and never took back out.

"Oh, uh, not too much. I meant to install one of those pot rack hangy-things but never got around to it. At least putting off that task didn't result in a life-changing event." I joke, embarrassed I forgot about my oven storage habits.

"Hmm," is all Hunter says as he removes the pots to the top of the stove and slides the frittata in.

"But to answer your question, no, I don't typically work this much on weekends. My weekdays can be long and hectic, but the weekend meteorologist typically covers holidays too. My boss pitched me an opportunity for an extra side gig they want to start. I'm going in to meet him this afternoon to talk more about it and needed to be prepared."

"Hmm," Hunter says again, then pushing a button on the oven until it beeps. He turns so his back is resting against the sink, his arms crossed. "I planned to wait until we were eating to launch into this, but you've added to my—we have some time until the frittata is ready. Can we sit?"

I glance at the small table behind me, covered with several weeks' worth of mail and outerwear. "Yeah, sure. Maybe on the couch?"

Hunter removes the towel from his shoulder, pulls two cans of something out of a bag, and follows me to the living room.

"So, now that you've seen the state of my kitchen and eating area, you've decided you don't want to do this anymore?" My words have the cadence and tone of a joke, but the open pit in my stomach waits for him to confirm the worst and bolt.

"What? No. Definitely not. It sparked something . . . Let me start at the beginning." He takes a deep breath. Maybe I'm not the only one who's nervous today.

"While I was in school, I sort of stumbled into a meal-planning business. One of the guys I worked out with at the gym complained about being bored of chicken and rice all the time, but didn't have time to do anything else. I had done some research on meals for myself and I thought they might work for him too, so I offered to share. He said if I put together meal ideas and a shopping list, he'd pay me a hundred bucks for two weeks." He cracks open one of the cans of sparkling water he brought over and takes a sip before continuing.

"Word spread through the gym, and soon, I had a handful of guys wanting me to do the same. I told them I wasn't a nutritionist, so couldn't personalize much, but lean proteins, high fiber—these gym guys ate it up. Word spread to their barbers, sisters, fellow church-goers, whoever, and suddenly, I had interest for other types of meals too. Since it was all local at first, I spent time learning the layout of the main grocery stores in the area, organizing the lists by aisle and section. Hayden's great with tech, so he helped me figure out how to create files people could upload into Instacart and DoorDash, get their groceries delivered."

"Hunter, that is really cool," I say, genuinely impressed.

"It is. I have a whole database of recipes now I've perfected —all stuff I'd be willing to cook and eat myself. My brothers, well, mostly Duncan, have been on me to see if I can scale it more. I haven't been so sure. It's a lot of time in front of a computer and not in a kitchen, like I imagined."

I nod. "I can see how it could balloon out of control. What does Duncan do?"

Hunter laughs. "Honestly, he takes people's money and makes them, and him, more money. At least that's what it seems like."

"Guess a business mindset is pretty engrained for him then."

He nods. "It is. Except he offered me start-up funding as a graduation present. I turned him down, telling him I knew it was a gift, not an investment. He makes so much money because he's successful, not because he gives handouts."

"So, now what?" I'm not following where this is headed.

"Well, now, everything has changed." His gaze falls to where my hand rests absentmindedly on my stomach, on our little Cumulus. "When I said I wanted to be involved, I meant it. That means, to me, I need to be here. In DC."

"You want to move to DC?" I say, a bit dumbfounded. He's right, it makes being involved a lot easier, but is a hell of a disruption to his life.

"I do. It's a big meeting day for both of us—I met with Duncan this morning to present my business plan. Hayden helped me put it together over the last thirty-six hours. Duncan says he needs to think it over, but I know he only said that because I made a big fuss about being treated like a normal client. So, I'll move here and hope I can launch in a bigger market, make it a full-time thing. Hayden's going to help me with an app . . . I hope I can be here permanently in two weeks."

"Two weeks?" I say, starting to panic. He's known about the baby for less than two days and he's ready to uproot everything. How can he be that sure?

"I know. I'll try to make it less if I can. But I need to sell my bike, give notice at a few places I've been picking up shifts, see if I can get out of my lease . . ." My hand on his arm causes him to trail off.

"Hunter, you don't have to do this. Or at least take some time to think on it first. Moving here, giving up your connections in kitchens, going full-time with the business, is that really what you want?"

Hunter slides his arm through my grip, tangling his fingers with mine. "If life's taught me anything consistently, it's we don't always get what we want. But moving here, being here for this baby, for you. If you'll let me, it might be what I need."

I stare at him in silence as he lets me soak it in, rubbing the back of my hand softly with his thumb.

"And a new dimension to the plan came to me after I got here this morning. What if I help you by cooking and meal planning for you? You said you don't cook much, and I saw the stack of sweetgreen napkins on the counter and the yogurt bowl from

South Block in the fridge. I know eating out isn't cheap, especially getting fresh and natural foods."

"I mean, I eat McDonald's too, but those napkins don't rat me out," I grumble. He laughs, giving my hand a gentle squeeze.

"I can supplement the Golden Arches, no problem. I originally planned to stay with Duncan or Hayden, but they're not super close to here, so maybe I can find a room for rent somewhere, to save time traveling back and—"

"Move in here." There goes that lack of filter again. But as soon as I say it, the pit in my stomach calms.

"What?" he says. It's his turn to look panicked.

"You're doing all of this for me, for us"—I press on my stomach again—"the least I can do is house you. If we're going to do this, let's go all in."

Hunter's eyes sparkle with something a lot like excitement. "If you're sure, that . . . that would be great. I want to be a part of everything you'll have me for. Morning sickness, cravings, doctor's appointments. All of it."

The air around us grows heavy as our eyes stay connected. His declaration rings in my ears, the sincerity and enthusiasm bleeding through. When Hunter says he's all in, it's not something he means lightly. I can tell. He'll be my person through this. I just need to let him.

The timer on the oven goes off, breaking the moment.

"I should get that," he says, giving my hand one more squeeze. I watch him walk to the kitchen, the sounds of frittata being removed from the oven and plated reaches my ears. I imagine a future where the sounds of someone else navigating my space is a normalcy, not a novelty. Eventually, the coos and cries of a baby join the fray.

Slow your roll, Lewis. Nothing is guaranteed.

Hunter brings a plate heaping with breakfast, handing it to me, along with the fork and napkin. Taking a bite, a groan leaves me, putting the purest smile I've seen yet on Hunter's face.

Guarantee or not, what will it hurt to enjoy the ride?

CHAPTER

Eleven

HUNTER

Thirteen weeks pregnant

My two-week timeline turned out to be a bit idealistic, but a little more than three weeks after I made Michelle breakfast, I'm crossing the boundary line into DC.

"I still don't understand why you got a U-Haul when you have like ten boxes, half of which are cooking supplies," Spencer complains for the umpteenth time in our ten-hour trip that unexpectedly took two days from Holly Ridge. We planned to make the whole drive yesterday, but trouble with the first truck I rented delayed us.

"You know, you didn't have to come with me." I grit my teeth and throw up a prayer as I navigate another roundabout on our way to Michelle's apartment.

"Spend two days of my two weeks off in a smelly truck and cheap hotel room with my favorite brother? I wouldn't have missed it."

I'd roll my eyes if I felt comfortable taking them off the road in front of me for even a second during the morning rush

84

hour traffic, but after twenty-eight years, Spencer knows it's implied.

We crawl forward and another light in front of us turns red, the traffic on the other side of the intersection stopping me from pulling through on the yellow. My grip on the steering wheel tightens and I check the clock for the fifteenth time in the last thirty minutes.

"Relax," Spencer says for the fourteenth time in the same span. "We're only a few minutes away. The appointment starts in thirty minutes. Hayden and Jax are already waiting outside the apartment. We'll get the truck unloaded and returned while you're at the doctor."

The less-than-ideal rush hour arrival is so I can make it to Michelle's second check-up. Spencer's not wrong about the overkill on the truck size, but neither of us has a car that can pull a trailer. Dad and Margaret offered to lend us their mini-SUV, but something about a thirty-one-year-old using his parent's car to move in with the woman he accidentally knocked up tasted sour, so here we are. They took the news of the pregnancy and my sudden move really well. Ninety percent of me knew they would, but the ten percent still stuck as the teenage screw up worried this would be the final straw that caused them to give up on me.

"Hunt, dude. Green light." Spencer points at the traffic light.

I pull the truck through, passing the delivery truck with his flashers on causing the bulk of the back up on this street and we start moving at a normal pace. Moments later, we're pulling up in front of Michelle's apartment and into the parking space she reserved for us through the city.

As Spencer promised, Hayden and Jax are standing in the shade created by the buildings this time of day. My heart rate picks up when I spot the red-haired figure completing their triangle. Michelle and I spent time coordinating and checking in over the past few weeks, but hadn't found a rhythm to talk about the more mundane and day-to-day things. I look forward to experiencing her day to day. It's funny how a person could go from someone you wistfully remembered to someone you found again and then to someone you'd miss in the span of a few days.

I hop out of the truck, tossing Spencer the keys over the hood. My hand moves automatically to Michelle's back. As she turns, I place a peck on her cheek, breathing in her smell. Even though my possessions are boxed up in a moving truck right now, I'm more settled than I have been since I left her the last time.

"Sorry. Traffic was fucking terrible. We need to go, yes?" I say, glaring over the top of her head at the shit-eating grin my twin sports. Like he doesn't worship the ground Charlotte walks on already. If they decide to have kids, he'll be an absolute wreck.

"The bus will be here in a minute, or we could walk. It looks like it'll be about twenty minutes either way with the morning rush," she says.

"If you're up for it, I'd rather not get in a vehicle again so soon."

Michelle nods. "Sure, it's not too hot yet today. You guys all set to unload?"

Spencer and Hayden hit identical salutes as Jax rolls her eyes. "I'll keep these two in line. You guys get going."

Michelle laughs as we set off toward the doctor's office. Halfway down the sidewalk, she shifts her bag to the shoulder closest to me, hefting its weight up higher.

"Here, let me," I say, gently tugging on the strap until she lets it slide off her arm and onto mine. "Sheesh, I didn't know meteorologists used bricks in their work."

"Wow. Dad jokes already. You're really leaning into the role," she says, deadpan.

I shrug, unable to keep the goofy grin from my face. "Gotta start sometime. But seriously, what all is in here?"

"Well, I have some notebooks. Shoes and a change of clothes for after my appointment. I'm hungry all the fucking time right now, so I packed some snacks. Plus, a water bottle because my pregnancy app yells at me about drinking water constantly. And there's a front moving through later today with a chance to produce severe storms and possibly tornadoes. There's nothing I can do for the tornadoes, but I packed a pair of sneakers in case of rain. It's going to be a hell of a day."

"Wow. That is equivalent to a few bricks, I think. What a weather day to welcome me to DC. How can you tell if the front has tornado potential, instead of only severe storms?"

Michelle launches into a complicated explanation about pressure, fronts, and wind streams, her hands gesticulating wildly. A lot of the terms she uses go right over my head, but I love seeing her so passionate. I make a note to find a good meteorological wiki and study up. I'd love to listen to her talk weather anytime.

Her explanation leads us the rest of the way to the doctor's office. The waiting room is packed when we step inside, even though it's not nine yet.

"Shit, it's busy. I'll go check-in—grab us those two seats over there? I don't see any others together."

I walk in the direction she pointed, speeding up as I see another guy approaching from the other direction. My butt hits the seat, with Michelle's bag in the one next to me while he's still five paces away. His eyes narrow, but he gives me a nod. I can tell when game recognizes game.

Women in a variety of ages and various potential stages of pregnancy fill the room. Some are sitting alone, others with partners. I think of Michelle sitting here alone for these appointments. In reality, I know she would have support if she needed it, but fuck, am I glad for barbecues, happenstance, and a touch of fate.

Michelle appears in front of me, and I move her bag so she can plop down. "One of the doctor's called out sick, that's the reason for the madhouse. I let them know my work shift starts in a little over an hour, but I know I'm not the only one trying to make it to work on time."

"Is the station far from here?"

"It's not too bad by bus. A bit of a stretch for a walk."

"If we need to, I'll order you a ride share."

"Or I can order my own ride share if I need to," she says, leveling me with a look. A look that reminds me Michelle has been living on her own for a long time, and while she's willing to accept me as part of this, she's not willing to entertain a hero complex. That's fine. I'll put away my lance and steed for a time when we need them.

"Lewis?" A voice from the door calls.

"That wasn't too bad," I say, trailing behind her as we pick our way through outstretched feet and strollers.

"Said from the perspective of someone who hasn't sat under an air conditioner in a thin exam gown waiting to have your vagina held open by cold metal." The nurse we pass at the desk through the door snorts.

"Am I right, or am I right?" Michelle says.

"Oh, you're right," the nurse responds.

"Understood. I'm a young Padawan in the gynecological world. I'm ready to learn and observe." I watch Michelle try—and fail—to stifle a laugh. Glad to know she appreciates my sense of humor.

We're ushered into a room where I stand along the wall while a different nurse takes Michelle's vitals and asks her questions. I see her making note of Michelle's morning sickness frequency and hope the doctor will address it. I have some questions of my own, but I'm getting the vibes I'm to be seen and not heard while we're in these walls.

The nurse grabs a cloth gown from under the exam table. "Go ahead and put this on. I see you requested an external ultrasound today, so I'll grab you a blanket too. Do you want your um . . ." the nurse's eyes flash to me, seeming uncertain of our relationship.

"Baby Daddy?" I helpfully interject, causing Michelle to groan and cover her face. Definitely a seen and not heard vibe now.

"This is Hunter. He is the baby's father and my new roommate. And yes, I'd like him to step outside."

"Let's go, Hunter," the nurse says. I follow her, reminding myself Michelle's clinical description of our relationship, while accurate, is meant to inform, not to hurt my feelings. All the same, I mentally move up a conversation about how our roommateship will proceed.

I hear the door creak behind me. Michelle peaks her head out. "You can come back in now."

I wait a beat to let her get away from the door and enter to see her climbing up on the exam bed, her legs covered in a sheet. We sit for a few minutes, the sound of people walking up and down the hallway on the other side of the door the only thing keeping us from sitting in complete silence.

"So, how's your new project going?" I ask, wanting to break the awkwardness. If our walk here proved anything, Michelle is always willing to talk about the weather.

"It's really great. We soft launched the blog last week and are going to film the first videos to post later this week. There hasn't been a ton of traffic yet, since we aren't promoting it anywhere, but the feedback we're getting is positive. It's great to have the chance to do the type of weather reporting I came to DC to do."

"What kind of reporting is that?" I ask, glad the tension in the air disappeared.

"Honestly, a lot like the stream of consciousness you got about storms and tornadoes on the way here. More scientific, more detailed. I started out with my forecasts trending in that direction but got some *feedback* viewers weren't connecting with me. I should have known; pretty, smart, *and* fat as a woman is too much for some people to handle."

"What?" I splutter. "You're, you're not . . ."

She holds up her hand. "Hunter. It's okay. The way I'm saying it, there's no derogatory meaning behind it. It's like saying you're tall, or someone else is thin. Being in an on-air position like I am means I've heard pretty much every opinion under the sun about my body. Growing up female in high school helped prepare me too. I'm healthy and I *love* my body."

I sit and absorb what she's told me for a moment, my eyes never leaving hers. I find myself nodding. "Okay. That's . . . that's good to know. It's going to take me some time to unlearn the way society uses the word more often, but I want to do it. Because, as you may recall, I loved your body too."

Michelle's cheeks tinge pink. "Breezing right past that for now. While we're on the subject, sometimes in places like this"—she indicates the exam room we sit in—"people will try to ascribe unhealthy connotations to the word. I have a lot of practice shutting them down, but I want you to be prepared."

I open my mouth to respond.

"Prepared to hear it. Not prepared to respond." She cuts me off. "I can handle it."

"Understood," I say. There's so much about this woman that amazes me. I can't wait to keep learning about her.

A knock on the door indicates the arrival of the doctor. A woman with brown hair walks into the room, and Michelle's face lights up.

"Dr. Barber," she says, her voice excited. "I didn't expect to see you again so soon."

"Hi Michelle," the doctor says warmly, sanitizing her hands from the station inside the door. "Dr. Patton is the one who called out sick today, so we're divvying up his morning appointments and rescheduling as many of the afternoon ones as we can." Her eyes move to me. "And who do we have here?"

"This is Hunter. He's the baby's father."

"Oh?" Dr. Barber's eyebrows shoot high on her forehead in surprise. I take that to mean Michelle explained a bit about our situation at her last appointment.

"It's a long story, but it turns out our social webs are a bit more tangled than we knew. He really wanted to be here today."

The doctor turns her warm smile on me. "Well, I'm glad you could make it, Hunter. Nice to meet you." Her attention returns to Michelle. "And now I understand the ultrasound request. To confirm, we can't guarantee your insurance will cover it. There's a chance, given your age, but we'll need you to sign a form confirming you'll pay out of pocket if you need to."

Michelle nods. "That's fine. I called the office ahead of time and got the cost. I'm good for it."

Dr. Barber smiles again. "Alrighty then. I'll go grab a machine and a tech, and we'll get you all checked out."

The door shuts softly behind her. Michelle takes a deep breath and then meets my gaze.

"You requested an ultrasound?" I say, my voice soft, like if I say it too loud, they'll cancel it.

She nods, swallowing hard. "I know you made a real effort to get yourself here in time for this appointment. I . . . I didn't want you to have to wait."

I cross to her side in two steps. Not a huge feat in a small exam room, but I know I would have gotten to her in the same amount of time in a room three times this size.

I reach out for her hand, and she lets me grab it. "Michelle, I . . ."

A knock sounds at the door again and her hand leaves mine, greeting the doctor and the nurse. I want to be a better listener, and I promise myself next time I'll bring a notebook. Get every little thing down and commit it all to memory. But right now, they sound like Charlie Brown's teacher as I wait until it's time for the little screen to turn on.

"Okay, everything from the internal exam looks great. Let's get you ready for the ultrasound."

My hearing flips on a switch, and everything seems too loud. The opening of the gel bottle. My heartbeat and breathing in my ears. The click of the machine being turned on.

This time, Michelle's hand finds mine, and she gives it a squeeze. The doctor puts the wand on Michelle's stomach. I watch the process in fascination until I hear it. A little "thump, thump" coming from the machine to our right.

"There they are. Nice and strong. Can you see it? It's that—"

"That little cloud right there," I say, pointing to the part of the screen that's flickering.

"That's right," Dr. Barber says. "Seems you've got good instincts."

"Little Cumulus," Michelle says, her voice wavering slightly. My eyes leave the screen to see moisture pooling in hers. I grip her hand tighter and follow those instincts, pressing a kiss to the top of her head.

"We'll give you two a minute," the doctor says, slipping out of the room after the nurse.

"Do you really think it looks like a cloud?" Michelle asks, her eyes locked on the screen.

"Absolutely, I do. The nickname fits them perfectly."

She leans her head on my shoulder, and we stay there together, looking at the life we somehow created flicker on the screen. Rightness washes over me again as I press another kiss to the crown of Michelle's head. However we decide to navigate this thing, I know we're doing it right. Together.

CHAPTER
Twelve

MICHELLE

Fourteen weeks pregnant

I t's taken some getting used to—having Hunter in the apartment. One lesson we both learned early on is to invest in some robes. Towel-clad run-ins on back-to-back days left me draining my vibrator of power the second night, hoping the buzzing wouldn't make it through the wall to Hunter's room. The extra-long shower I heard him take the next morning let me know I might not be the only one suffering.

I know we need to discuss what we are to each other—and soon. But I don't know what I want. Well, okay, equal parts of me want to climb him like a tree *and* maintain a functional co-parenting relationship with someone I've only known for a month. Those same parts of me disagree on whether those desires are mutually exclusive.

What I am sure of is Hunter is a fan-fucking-tastic cook and I've never eaten better in my life.

I'm climbing the stairs to my—our—unit on a Tuesday night after the type of very long day quickly becoming my norm.

Today included my normal forecasting shift, along with publishing a blog post and video about the incredibly active week Tornado Alley has seen. No one in the country has been able to escape news of the devastation and the posts are already getting more traction than anything I've done so far. I'm glad I decided to ask forgiveness and not permission to include links to fundraising efforts for those impacted.

I push open the door and the smell of melted cheese smacks me in the face, making me groan and drop my bag on the spot.

"You're back!" Hunter exclaims. He sounds genuinely happy to see me every time I walk through the door. He claims he leaves the apartment while I'm out, doing recon of grocery stores for the app or meeting with Hayden or Duncan about business stuff. I take a big sniff of whatever deliciousness he's whipped up for today, guilt spreading through me even while my stomach growls.

"Food will be ready in three minutes." It hasn't gotten old yet how he's able to time each recipe from my departure at the station.

I sit at the table, worried if I go to my room to change, I'll end up on the bed and miss out on whatever smells so delicious. Regret fills me almost instantly when the waistband of my pants cuts into my stomach. My day-to-day clothes aren't going to cut it much longer. One of the momfluencers I started following suggests using a hair tie looped through the buttonhole to give you another inch or so. I'll have to try it tomorrow.

"Here we are," Hunter says, setting a plate down in front of me, as well as one at his spot. His forearms are bare, hair mussed from the heat off the stove, and yet, the most alluring part is the tea towel draped over his shoulder. A different type of hunger fills me.

"What? You're not off chicken, are you? I mean, it's fine if you are, I can make something—"

"No, no, it smells delicious." I cut him off, guilt doubling at the thought he's doubting his food while I drool over the man presenting it.

Do I have a right to drool over him? I don't even know.

Hunter is still standing there, looking at me expectantly. Shit. "Oh, you know, the novelty of actually eating at the table, with placemats and everything." He smiles, heading to the stove, checking the burners are off. He leaves the towel behind and sits next to me.

"I did find these placemats in my room, you know. So, you either bought them, were gifted them, or were reverse robbed." Hunter's staying in the second, much smaller bedroom. I had done some consolidating when we thought Jax would be staying here for more than one night, but who knows what other treasures he might find. The room will eventually become the nursery, but we'll cross that bridge when the water gets high enough.

"My money's on reverse robbed," I say, before taking the first bite of food and letting out a moan I have no chance of containing.

Hunter's eyes darken slightly, but his tone is light. "You think it's good now, but you're missing out on how this wine compliments the sauce." He pours himself a glass of wine while I look sadly at my water glass.

"That's just mean. It's payback for the moan, isn't it?"

He winks in return and then digs in himself. We fall into a comfortable silence, though my mind races. Why can we joke so easily, but we can't talk about what we are to each other?

"So, I had something I wanted to ask you about," Hunter says, setting his fork down.

Is he a mind reader? I mirror him, keeping my hands empty. "Sure, what's up?"

"So, my parents, well, my dad and stepmom, Margaret, are wanting to visit all of us here in DC. They were thinking of visiting over the 4th of July."

So, not a discussion about us. Got it.

"That's nice—you all have made it easy on them congregating in the same place."

Hunter laughs. "That's what Margaret said. They also . . . they were hoping to have a chance to meet you. I know it's less than two weeks away, but I'd like for them to meet you too."

My heart warms at knowing I'm not some secret Hunter is trying to keep hidden. I didn't think shame matched his style, but confirmation is comforting. "So, they know about all the reasons you made the move?" I wondered what he told them when he announced his move, but knowing how much I hate talking about my relationship with my mom, I didn't want to pry.

"Yeah, I didn't want to lie to them. They took it well. I found out my mom and dad got married a week after finding out she was pregnant with Duncan. They had been together for a while by then, so different, but he got it."

I nod, piecing together bit by bit Hunter's family dynamic.

"It would be great to meet them. I found out today my boss got me access to watch the fireworks from the Post Office Tower for my post on how the weather impacts viewing fireworks. He mentioned I could bring a person or two . . . I'm not sure I could get the okay for everyone, but the four of us seems likely. Would they like that?"

The only word to describe Hunter's expression is beaming. "That would be amazing, Mich. Would your mom want to come too?"

Hunter's face falls, matching the shuttering I know my expression just did.

"Sorry . . . do you not . . ." He trails off, not knowing the end of his sentence.

I take a deep breath in. "I think I told you, my mom and I have a difficult relationship. Several therapists have helped me to recognize she sought validation from men and nowhere else, leading to some questionable parenting decisions, and some world views she's tried to pass on to me about men and their reliability. It is hard to be around her."

Hunter reaches out and squeezes my hand before returning it to his side of the table. I wish his reassuring warmth lasted longer.

"So, I'm guessing she doesn't know about the pregnancy."

I bark out a laugh before I can stop myself. "Sorry. No, she doesn't. And it's not because I'm ashamed of you, or us, or our situation. But I can hear everything she would say about you, about us, and about our situation. And I don't need that right now. I know I'll have to tell her eventually, but not now." I let out a quivering breath, pieces of hair framing my face fluttering upward with the force.

"I got it. Well, if you need me there when you do tell her, say the word. How about some ice cream for dessert?" He stands up, clearing our dishes. I marvel at yet another instance where Hunter read the situation perfectly—I desperately needed a subject change and ice cream is one of my favorite methods of self-soothing.

"That sounds great. Are you going to let me do the dishes tonight?" I ask. I've always heard if you cook, you don't clean, which seems fair. But so far, Hunter has insisted on taking up both roles.

"Did you post more than one thing on the blog today?" he asks, depositing a bowl of chocolate peanut butter in front of me.

"Yes . . ." I say, scooping a huge bite into my mouth, brain freeze be damned.

"Then you worked harder than I did. I've got this."

I suspect he would have claimed I worked harder than he did if all I accomplished in a day is getting out of bed to grab a new book from the bookshelf. I'll have to find something I can do for him soon, but I don't have it in me to argue tonight. I'm exhausted.

"Oh, one of the grocery stores I went to today had that

bubble bath you like on sale, so I grabbed a bottle. I saw you were running low. Feel free to leave your bowl on the table when you're done and go relax."

"You mean the bubble bath I've only ever found at Ulta and nowhere else and rarely goes on sale?" I lift an eyebrow in his direction as I take the last bite of ice cream.

He turns around, a smirk on his face. "Yup, that bubble bath. Must have been an ordering mistake."

I shake my head at him, knowing we both know he's lying. "Well, thank you. That's very thoughtful. A bubble bath does sound perfect." Especially if I sneak my waterproof bullet vibrator into the bathroom in my robe pocket. Running water should cover the vibrations. Turns out acts of service are just as potent with these pregnancy hormones as towel-clad run-ins. We learn new things every day.

HUNTER

Fifteen weeks pregnant

Being nervous is a new experience for me. Okay, well that's not entirely true, but being nervous for my parents to meet a woman? Definitely new.

I look at Michelle, straightening the throw pillows on the couch. Then she moves to the kitchen counter, sliding the charcuterie board I put together an inch to the right. I do my best to stifle a smile. This is the third time she's made this circuit in the last five minutes. Last time, it was two inches to the left. Next, she'll ask me if I think the pictures on the wall are crooked.

"Is this straight? I don't think it's straight." Right on cue.

"Mich, it's fine. My parents are not fancy people. They're going to love you."

She scoffs, heading back to the couch. "Yeah, right. Who loves the woman who manages to get knocked up by their son?"

I walk toward her, taking the throw pillow out of her hand and guiding her to sit down next to me. "It took both of us to

99

make this baby." My eyes follow the path her hand makes to rest on her stomach. "And they're going to love you because I—"

"I swear to god if you tell me you love me right now, Hunter Brandt."

A laugh escapes before I can stop it and she throws me a death glare.

"Sorry, sorry. I don't think we're that much of a cliché. What I was going to say is because they know you and the baby are important to me."

Michelle's face relaxes into a pleased smile. "It's not like I don't know that. You moved your whole life here, sold your motorcycle, bought me bubble bath last week. But it's still nice to hear out loud."

I make a mental note to tell her something I like or appreciate about her more often.

She looks around the room, her eyes analyzing for anything out of place. "Maybe I should light a candle? Does it smell funny in here? It smells funny—"

"Hey," I interrupt her spiral once more. The full weight of her gaze connects with mine. Those nerves from earlier? They're back with a vengeance, but for a whole new reason.

"Along with being important to me, I like you as a person, you know." *Wow, Cyrano. That's the best you can do?* "What I'm trying to say is you're important to me for more than carrying our baby. And because of that, I want to be sure I introduce you to my parents in the best way I can."

A puzzled look crosses her face. "So, you need to know my middle name or something?"

My hands have to be darkening the couch cushions by now. They're sweating so much. "No, well, yes, I'd love to know your middle name. I'd love to know everything about you, honestly. But in this case, I mean—what are we? How do I refer to you?"

"Oh." She pauses and looks thoughtful. "I guess 'baby mama' may not go over well with all crowds."

Emotion rises up in me to hear her say it again. "You are more to me than—"

"I know, I know," she cuts me off, her tone soothing. "I'm more to you than a human incubator. I'm sorry. I make bad jokes when I get nervous."

I think back over the past few weeks. "Just when you get nervous? Because I'd say you're pretty corny most of the time."

There's a pause before she speaks, her words soft. "Or do you make me nervous most of the time?"

I suck in a breath. Fuck. Did I force my way into her life? Is she not comfortable in her own home anymore?

"Your thoughts are all over your face, Hunt. I love having you here. But since you asked what we are . . . that's part of what makes me nervous. Beyond being future co-parents, I feel . . ." She straightens her shoulder and breathes deep. "I feel a pull toward you. I felt it that first night, in the days that passed even before I knew about little Cumulus here. It's not going away. And that terrifies me, because I know I should be putting the baby first, and maintaining a civil relationship between us is more important than any urges or instincts I have."

I waggle my eyebrows, breaking the tension. "So, you're having urges?" She smacks my arm gently.

"C'mon, you started this. What about you? Do you feel . . ." she trails off, looking lost. I curse my inability to be an adult— *again*.

"Yes. Yes, I feel a pull too. That's why I wanted to talk to you about"—I gesture around—"us, our situation, everything. If there's a chance for us to be more than co-parents and friends, I'd like to talk about exploring that."

She laughs, leaning back on the couch, her hand once more drifting to her stomach. I see her falling into the position absentmindedly more and more. It warms my heart each time.

"We're doing this all backward," she says. "Have a baby together, move in together, now try to define the relationship? I think we missed a few steps."

"Yeah, I feel like an engagement should have been in there somewhere."

"Let's leave the fake engagements to your brother, okay?"

"You know, there's something to that. We may not know how to define ourselves, but at least we don't have to tell my parents we faked an engagement."

We laugh. "No, we can definitely leave that honor to Preston and Jax," she says.

A comfortable silence descends, a feeling of home taking over as the refrigerator kicks on with its now-familiar hum and the smell of fresh bread the neighbors brought home from the farmers' market wafts in from the hallway.

"You know, you forgot something in your synopsis of our history," I say.

"What's that?" She rolls her head along the back of the couch to look at me.

"There were some corny pick up lines, some laughter, and some really great sex."

Her eyes grow serious. "I haven't forgotten. I think about it all the time. But that's what scares me. I think given where this is headed in twenty-five weeks, I need more than only laughs and good sex. We know those work. I need to know how things can be between us outside of those parts."

I lean forward slowly, letting her know I'm coming into her space. I rest my forehead against hers, wanting her to see me. Hear me. "I'm beginning to realize anything you want that's in my power to give, it's yours. Maybe outside, too."

We sit still, breathing the same air, tension building again, but this time tension of anticipation. Of want. Of fear. Of risk.

A buzzing noise slices through the air, the intercom. Michelle jumps away from me, and in the next second is on her feet. "Is that them?"

I look at my watch, seeing the rest of the morning has flown by. "Yup, right on time. Margaret's specialty."

"Shit! I never lit that candle. Can you buzz them in?" She

takes off for the kitchen, in search of matches. I watch her with a small smile on my face. I knew she felt it too, this *something* between us. We just need to be brave enough to explore it.

I push up and hit the button by the door. "Hello?"

"Hunter! It's us." I hear my dad's voice and my smile grows bigger, excited to have so many important people all in one place for the weekend. "Come on up," I say, pushing the button to unlock the front door.

I didn't show Dad and Margaret how much I appreciated their support and patience while we still lived in the same state. The nervous feeling returns. I meant it when I said they'll love Michelle. Pretty sure it's impossible not to. This time, the nerves accompany a desire for their approval. I'm finally taking chances, trying to be there for someone else and putting myself second. Hopefully, they can see it too.

Michelle moves into my view, setting a three-wick candle on the coffee table. She wafts the air above it. "I hope they can't smell the match . . ." She worries aloud, wringing her hands.

"C'mere," I say, waving her into my side. I kiss the side of her head. "Thank you for doing so much to make them feel welcome. I think it's going to be a great visit."

She looks up at me, a pleased smile on her face, her shoulders relaxed for the first time all morning. They press up toward her ears again as there's a knock on the door.

Before I let her go, I need to say one more thing. "Also, after they leave in a few days. I think we should go on a date." With that, I step away to open the door.

"Hunter!" Margaret exclaims, holding a bouquet of flowers and a reusable bag full of who knows what. She thrusts the flowers at my dad, so she has a free hand to give me a hug. It took me a long time to accept her hugs after she and my dad got together. She never pressed me or made me feel bad about it, but in the tightness of her squeezes now, I sense the desire to make up for those years when she had to love on me from afar.

"Hi, Margaret. Dad," I say next, the bouquet of flowers

tapping me gently on the back as Dad gives a hug of his own. "How was the trip down?"

"Oh, you know the train," Margaret says. "We got in later than expected last night, but Duncan had a car waiting for us. The hotel is too much, but that's your brother."

"I'm pretty sure the hotel and car are to make up for your insistence on taking the train," I say. "He would rather you let him fly you, first class."

"Psh, I know. I did enough flying everywhere when I worked. Now, I want to take my time, enjoy seeing the world around me." Margaret was a fierce businesswoman, having a stake in several patents she sold off when she retired. Now, she refuses to give up her more leisurely travel methods if she can help it.

A cough sounds from behind us. Michelle has a horrified look on her face when I turn around and I can only imagine she needed to cough for real but is afraid we think she was trying to remind us she's here. Like I could ever be unaware of her presence when we share a room.

I step back to stand next to Michelle. "Michelle, this is my dad, Stephen, and stepmom, Margaret. Dad, Margaret, this is my Michelle." She looks up at me in surprise, but I simply squeeze her waist. I didn't stop to think when it came time to make the introduction. Now I know she's open to more, I don't care what word falls between. As long as she's mine.

CHAPTER
Fourteen

MICHELLE

Seventeen weeks pregnant

> *Mich,*
> *Throw on something comfy. We'll be walking a little bit and be outside, but with airflow.*
> *I'll be back at 5:30. We'll leave then.*
> *Hunter*

I read the note over once more, excitement tingling in my stomach. Wait, was that excitement? I pause for a second, hand on my stomach, hoping it isn't the beginnings of the second trimester morning sickness I read about on the bus this morning. After a beat, I'm more certain of my excitement assessment and go to my room to change.

Right after Hunter's parents' visit, the winds shifted and smoke from wildfires in Eastern Canada started to float into the atmosphere of the East Coast. This meant diving into extra posts and videos for the station's weather blog, sharing apps to check air quality, interviewing experts, recommending masks, and keeping folks updated. Typical American attitude, not paying any attention until something impacts us.

With all his busyness, Hunter hadn't mentioned the idea of us going on a date again. At least I assume that's why it didn't get brought up and not because he changed his mind. But the winds had shifted again over the weekend, and last night, he asked for my schedule in the evenings this week.

It feels a little silly, to be so eagerly anticipating spending time outside the apartment with someone I spend hours with everyday *inside* the apartment. I decide not to examine it too closely and get changed. Some relief from the oppressive DC humidity also arrived today, right on schedule with my forecast from last week. Still, with a human inside me the size of an orange, I seem to experience temperatures in a different way than the rest of the world. I'm a little nervous about spending so much time outside, but given Hunter's promise of airflow and the sun setting in a couple hours, I'm ready to risk it.

I'm examining my outfit of black biker shorts and tank top, trying to decide what to do with my hair when the door opens at the front of the apartment.

"Hello?" Hunter calls.

I look at the clock on my bedside table. "You're seven minutes early. I'm *not* late."

He appears in my doorway, hands behind his back. "You'd be worth the wait, but you're right. Trains and cross walks were in my favor."

"What grocery stores did you map out today?" I ask, moving past him into the bathroom. He angles his body to keep his back out of my sight.

"I did a few in Chinatown this afternoon. I needed to swing by Duncan's office to grab our tickets for tonight."

I stick my head into the hallway, noting how pleased Hunter looks. "Tickets?"

"Here." He holds out what's in his right hand toward me. I take the bundle of blue and red cloth. The curly W on both items comes into focus.

"Nats gear. Are we going to a game?" I say, my excitement rising to meet Hunter's.

He nods. "We are. We're using Duncan's seats on the suite level. I bought the hats so we'd have some team spirit, but he had the jerseys waiting when I stopped in." He rolls his eyes in the fond way you have when a loved one is predictably over the top.

"Walk a bit, outdoors, but with airflow. I should have guessed a Nats game," I say, fitting the hat on my head and shrugging on the jersey. Hair question solved. "I can't believe Duncan has tickets available on such a short notice."

Hunter has put on his jersey too, and my eyes are drawn to the way the red sleeves offset the bright colors of the tattoos covering the rest of his arms.

"What's this one?" I ask, pointing at a tattoo near his wrist I haven't heard the story about yet.

"Well, it's a humpback whale," he says, his eyes glancing up to meet mine, before looking back down at the tattoo.

I nod. "I assumed an aquatic mammal, but didn't want to guess the wrong one. Is there a story behind it?"

Hunter keeps his eyes on the art, a whale under crashing waves, his finger stroking across it once. "Humpback whales communicate via these haunting and eerie songs. Some scientists are pretty sure they're for mating. Sometimes they sing near where they're feeding. There's probably a lot we'll never know about what they're trying to say. I've felt a lot like that at some points. I'm communicating but haven't found the right person to listen to me. To understand."

He looks up at me, his eyes open and vulnerable with the parts of him he laid bare for me. Mine start to water with the trust he's showing me.

"That's really beautiful. I'd . . ." I take a deep breath in, wanting to return his vulnerability with some of my own. "I'd like to learn your whale songs. Find out what they mean."

We stand in silence for a moment, our eyes locked.

After a beat, Hunter clears his throat. "We should probably head out."

I nod. "Sure thing. Let me go grab my belt bag."

As I walk toward my room, I hear him mutter. "Thank God."

"What?" I ask, slinging the bag strap over my shoulder and walking past him again to head to the door.

"Oh, I thought it would be criminal if your jersey covered your ass in those shorts. Luckily, it doesn't."

My back still facing Hunter, my cheeks pinch from the smile that breaks across my face. I school it into something hopefully resembling scolding when I turn around to face him. "You talk to all your first dates with that mouth?"

"First? This is our third date," he says, locking the door behind me as we start toward the Metro.

"How do you figure?" I ask, adjusting the bill of my hat, wishing I'd grabbed my sunglasses.

I look up and Hunter is holding said sunglasses out to me. "Well, the night we met has to count as date one. I did cook you a meal." I laugh and he continues. "And then the night you told me about little Cumulus, definitely date number two. Possibly even more memorable." He grabs my hand as we enter a cross walk.

"Date number three it is then," I say, and give up on containing my grin when I see Hunter sporting a matching one.

"I knew you'd see it my way." He lets me onto the escalator taking us down to the Dupont Circle Station first and stands behind me. I turn to look at him as we descend underground. The late-afternoon sunlight glows around his outline, and I'm thankful once more he grabbed my sunglasses. I can't seem to look away.

★ ★ ★

"I'm just saying, if every team raced something during the game, it would really bring something to the in-person experience," I say as Hunter unlocks our front door after the game.

"We watched two Cy Young winners engage in a pitching duel, and you're still focused on the racing presidents?"

"I mean, is it really a duel if there are no shots fired? There weren't any hits until the eighth inning. That's boring!" I drop onto the couch and accept the bottle of water Hunter hands me a moment later. I take a few swallows before saying, "You're right. The cotton candy was a mistake."

He laughs. "I'll always support you to eat whatever you want. It seemed a little dicey mixed on top of the loaded tater tots, nachos, and ice cream."

"I'll blame Cumulus for the spun sugar. They couldn't pass up a food that looked light and fluffy, just like them. Though to be honest, they wanted the nachos and ice cream too."

"But the tater tots?"

"Oh, those were all for me," I say with a laugh before drinking more water. "Thanks for getting me this, by the way."

"Of course," he says. "I'm sorry you didn't have a better time." A flash of disappointment crosses his face.

I sit up. "What? I had a great time."

"You did?" He looks uncertain. "But you thought the game was boring, and now you don't feel well, and—"

"Hunt," I say, leaning toward him. "I'm seventeen weeks pregnant. I can feel crappy after ten hours of sleep and spending the day sitting on the couch. And the game being so low scoring allowed me to do more people watching. If it didn't, I would have never spotted that couple."

He smiles at the memory. "I can't believe you called he was going to propose. The way they were fighting the whole game, I thought they were more likely headed for a break up."

I shrug. "Maybe fighting is foreplay for them. She seemed pretty enthusiastic about her yes." I laugh at the memory of her jumping into his arms and spilling the beer of the guy sitting behind her.

"But, back to the point," I say. "I had a great time. You planned something special for me, made sure it was somewhere I would be comfortable, and supported my questionable food choices, even trying to save me from myself. Great third date." I meet his eyes at the end and hold them for a moment.

He breaks the eye contact first. "Well, you have an early morning, and I've got a meeting with Duncan and Hayden at nine. Can I walk you to your door?"

I look behind me at the front door locked and dead bolted behind us before looking back at him. "That door?"

He shakes his head before offering me his hand and helping me off the couch. "No, that one." He jerks his thumb at my bedroom door.

"Oh, well then, of course. What a gentleman," I tease as we walk down the hallway hand in hand. Any trace of humor dies in my throat when I meet his gaze at the entrance to my room. His eyes are dark and serious.

"Thank you for tonight. I know we hang out here a lot, but I loved being out, laughing with you, throwing dirty looks at other guys who checked out your ass."

The humor returns as a laugh bubbles up. "They did not."

He nods solemnly. "They did. You don't have eyes in the back of your head, so you can't see. My caveman brain says next time I'll get a jersey that covers your ass, so I'm the only one who gets to see it, here in our home. But my more rational brain says I could never dull the way you shine."

I'm left speechless as he reaches up to spin my hat so the bill is at the back of my head, matching his. He leans down slowly and my eyes close right before his lips brush mine, once, twice, and then they're gone. I lean forward trying to chase the contact, my eyes blinking open as I rock back flat onto my feet.

"Goodnight," he says, his hand tracing down my arm, squeezing mine once before trailing his fingers across my palm and walking to his room, the door closing behind him. I stare at the closed door for a moment before going about my nighttime routine, unable to forget the way it felt when his lips brushed mine. Of course, I've felt his lips there, and many other places before, but this was different. This time, he knows my name, my favorite foods, how I sound when I sing in the shower.

Later, when I'm in bed for the night, I hear his door open again and realize he waited to head into the bathroom, so it would mirror the end of a date between two people who don't sleep with only a wall separating them.

I brush my hands over my lips with the same feather light touch Hunter used earlier.

This time, he kissed me like it meant more.

CHAPTER

Fifteen

MICHELLE

Twenty weeks pregnant

As the fourth episode of *The Property Brothers* begins in the waiting room and my stomach grumbles its loudest growl yet, I wonder how exactly a gestational diabetes test isn't considered a form of torture condemned as a crime against humanity. But that's probably the fact I haven't eaten anything since last night.

Luckily, I'm almost at the end of the process, waiting for the results of the third hour blood draw, and then I can get something to eat. Hunter mentioned District Taco or Falafel, Inc. or both if I can't decide once I'm given the okay to eat again.

Given my pre-pregnancy weight, the current size of the baby and my "advanced age," the doctors recommended I do my glucose tests at twenty weeks. My results were barely in the range for failing the one-hour test, so I'm back for more. If things are negative this time around, they might have me do the one-hour test again at twenty-eight weeks and determine next steps from there. I shudder at the idea of having to drink the glucose solution again in two months, but whatever Cumulus needs to stay healthy.

An upbeat jingle sounds from the TV in the corner, two carrots singing and talking about an erectile dysfunction medication. Ironic, considering the events bringing so many of us into this waiting room.

Not that I know much about Hunter's current erectile function levels. But based on my multiple experiences over the course of those initial ten hours . . . I'm starting to think it might be worth getting an updated baseline.

We've gone on a few more dates since the baseball game. Nothing quite as elaborate, especially since the city is in the middle of a record high heat wave. Still, the intentional time Hunter's been planning for us to spend together, whether working through the list of restaurants he's cultivated since his move or in an icy movie theater watching a rom-com he enjoys as much as I do, has been nice.

The air in the waiting room changes, and I look to the door to see Hunter standing just inside it, looking for me. A smile lights up his whole face once he spots me and moves through the crowded room of babies and pregnant individuals. My chest warms at seeing him arrive. I told him not to change the feedback session he and Hayden had scheduled with app beta testers for this morning, since the first few hours consisted of me sitting around and getting poked. He insisted on being here for the final results with the doctor though, as well as making sure I got fed immediately afterward.

"Hi," he says as he plops in the chair next to me, pressing a kiss to my cheek.

"Hi," I say back, squeezing his knee affectionately. Gosh, he looks handsome. And that's not only the glucose test hunger talking. It's like I summoned him with my thoughts of his penis. Nothing has progressed physically, which I know has a lot to do with my comments earlier in July. But I'm getting to the point where I want to start mixing the new closeness we're finding with the stuff we know already works.

His presence calms a part of me worried about the results. Hunter's been doing research on adjustments to make to his meals for us, if need be, and knowing I won't navigate the results alone is a relief.

"So, what kind of grey and neutral decorating scheme have the brothers developed today?" Hunter asks, right before the call of "Lewis?" comes from a nurse in pink scrubs.

"Luckily, it's very grey and very neutral," I say as we walk toward her. "You didn't miss anything."

We follow the nurse into an exam room, where she tells us the doctor will be in to talk to us soon.

"Who are we seeing today?" Hunter asks. His hand falls on the uterus model sitting on the desk before he realizes what he's touching and pulls away.

A giggle escapes. "Careful, we wouldn't want to be known as the couple who spills things on the floor most times we're here. We're seeing Dr. Jameson. It was supposed to be Dr. Simon, but I guess things got switched around. I couldn't get enough service to look up Jameson, so I guess we'll see."

Hunter's staring at me, eyes wide.

"What's up? Oh no, have I had glucose solution on my face this whole time and no one's told me?" I rub next to my mouth.

He shakes his head. "No, you called us a couple . . ."

I open my mouth to respond but knuckles rap on the door before I can.

"Come—"

The door pushes open before I can finish my sentence and my stomach plummets as a man about my age enters the room. He takes one look at me, his eyes tracking to Hunter's tattoos, before he sighs with a haughty air.

"Dr. Jameson. You're Michelle Lewis?"

"Yes," I say, uncertainty lacing my tone.

"I see you're here for your three-hour gestational diabetes

test. I'm going to assume given everything"—he gestures at all of me—"the results are going to be positive for this one as well, but I'll go grab the labs. Be right back."

Hunter looks between me and the door in shock, all memory of the conversation the doctor interrupted blown away. "Did he really just? He can't . . . I mean, he's here to help you, and then he . . ." Hunter continues to have his head implode at the doctor's introduction.

I blow out a shaky breath, forcing myself to breathe in and out at a normal pace. Fuck. "He can. Welcome to fatphobia in the medical community."

"But he didn't look at your file to know your blood pressure, previous blood work, everything else is healthy. Plus, he would know plenty of people fail the one-hour test and have normal results with the three-hour." Like I said, he's done his research.

I try to appear nonchalant, sensing Hunter is getting worked up, and I don't want him to know how much this still rattles me, even after almost forty years. "For some people, appearance tells them everything they want to know."

"Well, I'm going out there, we can see another—"

Another knock at the door, followed by an immediate re-emergence of Dr. Jameson, cuts him off. The doctor shuts the door behind him, almost hitting the nurse following him into the room in the face. Her carefully neutral look tells me everything I need to know about this guy. He's an asshole, and everyone knows it. I better buckle in.

"Well, *somehow*, your glucose numbers are in a normal range. You're sure you fasted all night and drank *all* the solution?"

Hunter moves next to me, and I sense his mouth is about to open, so I grab his wrist. "Yes, I'm sure. I was happy to follow your practice's recommendation and take the tests early, but I'm not surprised by the results. Especially during my pregnancy, we've been following—"

"Hmph." He cuts me off. Hunter's arm grows tenser under my hand. "I'm not interested in your home remedies. I'm surprised you got pregnant in the first place, given your advanced age and"—he makes a gesture indicating to everything about me again—"but I guess luck is on your side. Now, about the weight you've gained since being pregnant . . ."

"Anything I've gained is within the norms of a woman for my BMI at twenty weeks," I say, trying to keep my voice strong. This asshat doesn't deserve to hear he's getting to me, cutting right to my core. I'd learned long ago weighing myself regularly isn't something that served me, so keeping closer tabs on it during this pregnancy is already grating on me.

"Well, that may be, but you'll never get it off again once you've given birth. I guess you can stop by the desk for some meal planning resources. I'm not sure they'll meet your appetite, though."

I recoil like I've been struck.

"Hey, buddy," Hunter says, his tone low and furious. "That's enough. You've told us what we need to know, so kindly get the fuck out."

"You can't talk to me like that." Dr. Jameson looks flabbergasted anyone would even dare.

"But you can talk to her like that? Big man in a white coat. You're lucky I respect the woman next to me enough to let her fight her own battles when she wants to. Wonder how that coat would look up against the wall?" Hunter's eyes flash, his meaning clear without actually threatening the other man.

The doctor's cheeks flush red, and he stands up taller, straightening his tie. "Well, if that'll be all, Jessica here will get your next appointment made." With that, he leaves the room.

The dark-haired nurse clears her throat. "Hi, I'm Jessa, actually. And I'm so sorry."

"He a fuck face like that all the time?" Hunter takes a deep breath. "I'm sorry. You're not responsible for his behavior."

She smiles gently. "He is a fuck face like that all the time. People have complained, but . . ."

"Because he's a presumably straight, white man, nothing

sticks," I say, my heart in my stomach. I've sat in these rooms in far less clothing than I'm in now, but have never felt more exposed.

Jessa mutters something under her breath in Spanish before raising her voice. "You didn't hear this from me, but I do think he's one or two complaints away from actual action. We've lost a lot of patients because of him. I can give you the names and contact info of where they go, if you'd like."

The weight of Hunter's gaze on me is like a tangible touch, knowing this is my call. "No." I shake my head. "I've been so happy with everyone else here, and I've dealt with judgments about my weight all my life. No guarantee someone else wouldn't do the same thing."

She nods, an empathetic look on her face.

"If we wanted to make a complaint to someone here, though," Hunter asks, casting a furtive look in my direction. I'm too tired to protest that I don't want to make any waves.

"I can get you that information too," Jessa says. "I'll be right back with the contact info and the details for your next appointment. Then you guys can get out of here."

A thick silence descends over the room after she walks away. I know Hunter's looking at me, waiting for me to meet his gaze, but I'm not sure what I'll see there. Worse, I don't know what he'll read in me.

"So, what did you decide about lunch?" Hunter asks after another moment.

"I'm not really hungry," I say, hating how the joy of our lunch plans has evaporated.

"Mich, you need to eat something. It's been over twelve hours." His voice is gentle, coddling even, and I snap.

"I *know* I need to eat something. But forgive me if my appetite is gone." His eyes hold mine as my voice shakes and a tear escapes. I regret lashing out immediately.

He studies me closely, his eyes searching my face, but betraying nothing at what he finds there. When he speaks, his tone contains no indication I just snapped at him for something that's in no way his fault. "How about we take a ride share home and I'll make you a smoothie? We have those blueberries I got at the farmers' market yesterday." The suggestion carries the same warmth and care he always shows when he wants to do something for me, to help me.

Still, the instinct to make myself as small and amiable as possible is too hard to fight. "We can take the bus, it's fine. And I'm sure you have other things to do. It's the middle of the day."

He steps closer and slowly reaches his hand toward my face, as if he expects me to pull away. I fight against the impulse. "Hey. That guy sucked. And I'm so sorry you dealt with that today and ever before. If I thought the idea of bodily violence appealed to you, and I wasn't positive he's the litigious type, I'd make good on my wall-smashing threat. But let me take you home, out of the heat, and make you a smoothie, okay?"

I nod, his hand cupping my cheek all the while. "Okay."

A few hours later, a knock on the door wakes me. "Hey, it's me." Hunter's voice comes through the door. "You told me not to let you sleep past four, but I also didn't want to wake you, so it's 4:30 now."

I rub my eyes, trying to shake off the disorientation that accompanies a solid mid-afternoon nap.

"Uh, you awake? Can I come in?"

Right. Open mouth, use voice. "Yeah, I'm up. Come on in."

Hunter walks through the door, and pauses a few steps inside, looking around. "Wow, I'm not sure I've seen it so dark in here since . . ." His voice, soft and low, gives me goosebumps.

The low lighting with the shades pulled suddenly looks more sexy than cozy. I push up against the pillows, keeping the blankets tight around my waist. My pant-less state is more obvious than normal.

"Oh, right. I guess we do spend most of our time in the living room." And pulling all the blinds this afternoon felt right to match my mood.

He nods, leaning against the dresser. "How are you feeling?"

All thoughts of sexiness leave my mind at the reminder of how the day started. Fuck, I hate he saw that, heard that. There's a good chance he'll see some pretty weird stuff by the time this baby is born, but that's natural. According to Dr. Jameson, there's nothing natural or redeeming about my size, and that cuts right to the core of me.

I shrug. "I'm okay, I guess. The nap was necessary." I play with the comforter in my lap, avoiding his eyes.

"I'm thinking of making burrito bowls for dinner. Penzeys sent some spices over, including a mix for taco meat, so I want to try it out."

"Sure, sounds fine. You know I'll like whatever you make."

"Yeah, but you didn't get your bowl this afternoon after the appointment, so I thought I could make up for it. I'm no District Taco, but I can whip up a mean queso."

I nod, still silent.

He stands there for a moment longer, the air heavy with intent on his side. I can tell he wants to say something else, but isn't sure what.

"All right then, I'll get working on food. Should be ready in about twenty-five minutes or so."

"I'll be out in a minute," I say. "I'm still waking up." I put on a smile that feels fake from tip to tip. The look on Hunter's face says he isn't much more impressed by it.

"No hurry. See you out there in a few."

He raps his knuckles twice on the top of my dresser and turns toward the kitchen. The apartment fills with sounds of him putting pans on top of the stove and getting ingredients out of the refrigerator.

Knock it off, Lewis. You love queso. You love yourself. You're not going to let a miserable asshole and his biases keep you down.

Maybe if I wash off the memory of the day before dinner, I'll feel better. I grab what I need from my room and set it in the bathroom before walking out to let Hunter know my plans.

His arms flex with the speed he chops peppers and onions on the counter. For a moment, I watch him, mesmerized by the skill and care he puts into simple tasks. I really should volunteer to help more, though the last time he had me cut something, he took the knife out of my hand two seconds later. Something about me needing all ten fingers for "Itsy Bitsy Spider."

He looks my way a moment later. "Hey there."

"Hi. Something smells good out here."

"New spices pass the smell test. Check." He gives me a soft smile. One that says he knows he's being over the top, but he'd love to see me smile too.

"I'm going to get a quick shower before we eat. Want to wash away the day."

"Definitely. Be sure you don't wash away your appetite." He winks, and I laugh.

"The dad jokes are becoming more regular, you know."

Shrugging, he says, "I'm not going to fight it. See you in a few."

As the hot water sluices over me, I let the lavender scent of my body wash unwind some of my tangled thoughts and the warmth undo some of the tension in my shoulders. Still, when I get out of the shower, my eyes avoid the mirror as I get dressed. Today is a day for being gentle, and tomorrow is a day to claw back my appreciation for all my body does for me, and now for little Cumulus. This is simply a setback.

I braid my wet hair in a long plait behind me, not wanting to bother drying it. If there's anyone who can make me feel better, just by sharing space, it's Hunter. My stomach growls for the first time since Dr. Jameson stole my appetite, and I head out to the kitchen to enjoy dinner.

CHAPTER
Sixteen

HUNTER

Twenty weeks pregnant

My knife sticks in the cutting board slightly with the unnecessary vigor I'm chopping these vegetables with. I put the knife down, grip the countertop, and hang my head. I want to wring that doctor's neck for not only his irresponsible bedside manner, but for the lasting impacts it's had on Michelle's mood. I know the confident, strong woman is in there, but I don't know what to do to help bring her back out. My tattoos bring their own sort of biases with them, but I know enough to know it's different.

Michelle comes out from the shower more relaxed than before it, but she still isn't her normal self. She sits across from me, a more genuine smile on her face than the bullshit she tried to pass off earlier. Still, her eyes are dimmed, her shoulders more sagged.

"So, tell me more about this Penzeys spice thing?" She's giving a masterclass in deflecting right now, keeping the conversation flowing in a direction opposite of her feelings.

I continue to play along, like I have all meal. "A client who signed up for one of the spots I'm keeping open while we wait for the app works at the Arlington store. She mentioned it to someone, so they sent me some spices to try out. They're interested in a meeting to see if we can work out a deal to have the spices default to theirs when the selected store sells them."

"Hunter, that's amazing." Her energy picks up to the highest it's been since she left this morning.

I shrug. "It's pretty cool, and their stuff is high quality. We'll see. I don't want to get my hopes up."

"Well, I think you should let those hopes climb a little bit. But I didn't know you were doing clients here? I thought that would wait until the app launched."

Shit, I forgot I planned on not telling her about taking on clients now.

"Just a few—I used referrals from my clients back in Holly Ridge, so I could keep it limited. Duncan keeps telling me to use some of his investment money for other expenses, but I'm trying to keep it limited to the app and company."

"Do you need more money from me for groceries? Or adjust our rent split? I paid the whole rent before you moved in, and you're saving me food money from my takeout habit, so—"

"*No*," I say, with more force than I mean to. "I mean, no, I'm okay. I still have my savings and what I got for my bike. I want to be sure I have a good amount of emergency savings." I've also been putting out feelers for kitchen subbing gigs as I get more connected with the food scene in DC, but I won't mention that either. I don't want Michelle to worry she'll be left on her own too much—I'm sure I can figure it all out.

She opens her mouth, ready to protest again about money, I'm sure. "Want anything for dessert?" I ask, grabbing her bowl that's been empty for a few minutes now. I set them in the sink, debating whether I should do the dishes now or carry on with Mission Raise the Mood. I turn around and catch Michelle's glum expression before she can fix her face. Mood mission it is.

"Want to watch a movie?" I ask.

"Oh, sure. I guess so." She moves over to the couch and covers herself with a blanket. To keep the humidity down, the AC is at a frigid level, especially when you're under a vent.

"Your choice," I say, sitting at the other end of the couch. After handing her the remote, I swing her feet so they're in my lap but still tucked in the blanket. Our dates the past few weeks have made us more comfortable with casual touch. One thing I've learned is Michelle loves a good foot rub, but hates her feet being cold. I worry she will pretend she doesn't want a foot rub, trying to make herself as unbothersome as possible. Ridiculous, she couldn't bother me if she tried.

"Oh, look, the movie with the Christmas stripper show to save the small town is in the top ten. I didn't get enough Christmas in July time in," she says, perking up again. After navigating to the movie in question, she presses play and nestles deeper into the pillows propped behind her back. Her feet wiggle in my lap, her signal she's ready to take advantage of their proximity to my hands. I smile and rub my hands together to ensure they're nice and toasty before sliding them under the blanket and working the arches of Michelle's foot.

We lose ourselves in the story. There's something comforting in the formula of boy meets girl, girl needs boy's help but doesn't want to ask, boy makes grand gesture to win girl's heart, and they work together to save the day.

"Mmm," Michelle says as the Christmas Revue scene begins.

"Is that noise sponsored by my excellent foot rubbing skills? Or that handsome man on the screen right now? Answer carefully," I tease, my tone light. In reality, I'm glad to hear her make a happy noise.

"Why can't it be both? I'm getting one thing I need from you, and something else I need from Mister Handsome up there." She juts her chin to the screen.

"Psh. I can do that."

The first laugh I've heard from her all day escapes. "You. Can do *that*?" She points to where the actor is essentially humping the floor, held up by one arm, before jumping right into a standing position.

"You wound me." She laughs harder. "Okay, I'm not sure I can do *that* exactly. But I've got moves."

"I'm sure you do," her voice teasing, but still laced with doubt.

"Okay, fine. You brought this on yourself." I snag the remote from her hand, pause the movie, and hand her my phone. "You can choose the music. I need to prepare myself."

I slide out from under her feet and stand up, moving the coffee table out of the way.

"Hunter, what—"

"Less scoffing, more song selecting," I say, directing her attention to the phone screen as I move one of the dining room chairs into the area I opened in front of the couch.

She scrolls, biting her lip in that way that drives me wild, before releasing it to laugh in triumph, the perfect song chosen. "Ready?" she asks. Her tone tells me she still thinks I'm bluffing. Little does she know the most convenient group exercise class for my schedule some days at the Winterberry Glen fitness center was Pole Dancing. My moves are for real.

Smooth saxophone starts to come out of the speaker. "Seriously?" I ask.

Michelle's whole body is shaking with giggles. "It's called 'Santa's Sexy Package.' I can't make this up."

After a few more beats, I decide to lean into it. "All right, we can work with this." I walk around the chair, sticking my ass out and shaking it in her face.

"Woo," she half yells. "Shake that money maker!" Laughter coats her voice. In this moment, I know even if I'd never danced with a chair in my life, I still would have found myself here because it's making her so happy.

I complete another circuit around the chair and drop into it.

I roll my abs as I unbutton my shirt, shrugging it off. If Brad Matthew Whatever gets to be shirtless, so do I.

Michelle's eyes widen as they trace my skin. "He . . . he doesn't have those tattoos." I watch her swallow. "It's a real missed opportunity on the part of the costume department."

I roll myself up out of the chair and Michelle pulls the blanket up to her cheeks with a squeak. I stop, dropping the act and plopping back into the chair. "What? Too much?"

She shakes her head no, then changes her mind and nods. "But in the best possible way. I . . . I thought it would be silly. Like on the TV. But fuck . . . you're hot." The rasp in her voice is one I haven't heard since March, since that first night. Shit, I think I went too far.

I lean down to pick my shirt up off the floor. "No!" I stop, bent in half. "I mean, if you want to keep going, I . . . I think you should." She looks down at my phone, types something and a familiar R&B beat starts playing instead.

The air changes. It ripples with something *more*. Something real. Something dangerous. I pause before reading the earnestness in Michelle's expression. I didn't want her to be sad anymore, right?

I come around from behind the chair and swing her feet to the floor. She lowers the blanket to her waist before whipping it off completely. I start to move in beat to the music, working myself closer and closer. I want to be sure she has plenty of time to say stop if she needs to.

Her eyes trace over me, heat rising in them. Teeth work her bottom lip, and without realizing I'm moving, my hand reaches out to gently pry it free.

She lifts her hands like she wants to touch me, but stops partway to my skin. Lost in the fantasy. "At our place, you have full permission to touch," I say. She runs her fingers down my abs, sending a shudder through me. Putting her fingers in my belt loops, she brings me down, straddling her legs.

"Oops," she says, not looking sorry in the least. I shift so more of my weight is balanced on my knees, but her legs still press against the inside of mine. She traces the artwork on my arms, just like she did that night.

"You're beautiful," she whispers, and in a moment, we're back to us. Bonnie and Clyde. Michelle and Hunter. Something that's felt out of rhythm for the past five months rights itself. But before I follow that instinct down . . .

I grab her chin, bringing her gaze to mine. My grip is firm enough so the words she hears in the next moment will carry their weight. "You are beautiful." As I expected, her eyes start to cloud over. "No. Listen. You are gorgeous. Captivating. Enchanting. Beguiling. God, I wish I had a thesaurus so I could give you more words. And there is nothing more in this moment I want to do than show you how much I mean this. But if you're not ready to hear it, to feel it? I want you to tell me. Because this day has sucked so fucking much and all I've wanted to do all day is give you whatever I can, whatever you need. So, tell me. Say the word and I'll start the movie again, rub your feet, whatever you want."

A moment passes and I worry once again, I'm too much. But then—

"Kiss me," she breathes, and in the next instant, my mouth is on hers. A groan escapes one, or both, of us as I sink my legs further into the couch cushions. Our tongues tangle, and I pour every instant I've spent wanting her since I last had her mouth into this kiss. I hope I'm reading the same from her.

Her hands travel down my back, into the waistband of my jeans. As her fingers grip my ass, my hips thrust forward involuntarily. "Mngh."

She sucks air in, pulling away. I see discomfort on her face.

"Fuck, what is it?" I scramble so I'm on my knees in front of her, removing my weight altogether.

Her face grows red. "Uh, your friend down there"—she nods toward my crotch—"pushed Cumulus right into my bladder. Ugh, so inconvenient." She covers her face in her hands.

"Hey," I say, pulling one hand down to hold in mine. She pops an eye open and meets my gaze. "We can pick this back up anytime you want. Straddling a pregnant woman probably wasn't my best move." I slide over so I'm out of the way.

"You're so nice," she says as she pushes herself up out of the couch. I offered to help last week and thought my dick would wither off from the look she threw my way. "Bodily functions really take the wind out of the sexy sails."

She takes care of the situation my rogue cock created, and I put myself and the living room back together. The same way I felt things heading somewhere, I know the moment has passed.

Michelle appears a moment later, standing against the wall where the hallway opens to the living spaces. "Look, Hunter . . . I think I'm crashing from everything that happened today, and . . ."

"You don't have to apologize. Not stopping the train to sexy town earlier, after the day you've had and when we haven't really talked about it, is my bad."

She bites that lip again. "You definitely got me out of my head there. Would you want to come and lay in bed with me? You don't have to stay all night if you want your space, but I think I'll fall asleep easier if you're there with me."

I step up and cup her face. "I'll be there all night long if it helps you sleep five minutes more." *You're getting better at this, Brandt.* But it's not a line. I mean every word. "Do you need in the bathroom?"

She shakes her head no, dislodging my hand.

"Okay. I'm going to duck in there, and I'll be right with you."

I stop in my room to change into a T-shirt and gym shorts. The less opportunity my cock has to go rogue again today, the better.

The scene waiting for me in Michelle's room makes my heart stutter in my chest. The same soft bedside lamp on for light. She's on her side, eyes closed, with the blankets pulled up to her chin against the cold air from the window unit. I bought and installed it after the third time she woke up sweaty. These old buildings don't have the duct work to support even AC distribution. She protested about the environmental impacts, so I promised we'd donate it to a women's shelter after this summer and buy some carbon credits. Worth every penny when I see firsthand how comfortable she looks.

I turn off the light and then walk around to the other side to slide in. My hip touches her backside, and I freeze, unsure how to proceed.

"Are you wearing shorts?" she murmurs, still facing away from me.

"Uh, yeah. I changed before I came in."

"I thought you couldn't sleep with clothes on."

When the fuck did I tell her that? "Can't sleep is a strong phrase. Plus, I want you to be comfortable."

"It would make me comfortable to feel your skin on mine. C'mon, big spoon."

I sit up to pull the shirt over my head and lift my hips up to slide the shorts off. I say a prayer to the God of Hard-ons to keep things PG. Well, as PG as it can be when you're almost naked in bed with someone else who—my bare legs brush against hers as I press myself against her back—is also almost naked.

"Hmm." She hums, sounding so content, it makes me wish I could tattoo a sound onto my body to keep it with me forever. Her breathing evens out almost immediately. I lay there in the dark wondering at what point my luck changed to bring me Michelle. And at what point I'll inevitably fuck it up.

Mentally shaking myself, I do my best to push those dark thoughts aside. Instead, I try to think of what I can do for Michelle to thank her for letting me be a part of this. As I listen to her breathe, an idea comes to me. Relief courses through me as I think through the plan, certain I'll remember it tomorrow because it's not for me. It's for Michelle. My Michelle. My eyes close, and I drift off.

CHAPTER
Seventeen

MICHELLE

Twenty-one weeks pregnant

I wake up more well-rested than I've been in weeks. The solid, warm presence at my back can claim credit. His hand is cupping my stomach, his breath even and warm at my ear.

After yesterday's appointment, my brain tries to revolt about anyone touching my belly, but my heart pushes back until I can conjure up thoughts to combat the negativity. Here is a man who cares so much for me, for us, for this baby we made together. Instead of discomfort, a sense of being cherished rolls through me.

To the outside observer, my shape hasn't changed much at this point. This means I've been able to keep it quiet at work, which I'm grateful for, especially with the opportunity of the web content. But Hunter, if he were awake, would notice a firmness is forming underneath my skin where his hand rests. The space Cumulus is occupying grows week by week.

Like they're responding to my thought process, a flutter comes from where Cumulus is resting. My eyes close again, wanting to extend the contentedness of the moment the three of us are sharing.

"Holy fuck," Hunter exclaims as my eyes pop open. "Was that . . ." Maybe he doesn't want to jinx it.

The firm nudging happens again, right where Hunter's hand is resting on my stomach.

"Yup, that was little Cumulus saying good morning." A giddy laugh follows as I move my hand to rest right next to his. He laces our pinkies together as we wait and hope for another kick.

"Has that happened before?" he whispers, like speaking too loudly will startle the baby.

"No," I whisper back, in case he's on to something. "I've felt small movements before, but it's the first time—"

I'm interrupted by one more kick and Hunter's the one to laugh this time. "Holy shit, there's a baby in there."

A full belly laugh erupts from me dislodging Hunter's hand. Moment broken, I roll over to face him, watching as the sheepish look on his face melts into laughter too.

We come down from the high slowly. Hunter continues to gaze at me with wonder, and I can't look away.

"That . . . that was amazing," he says. "I can't believe I got to be a part of it."

I reach up and stroke his face, my hand tracing down his chest until I clasp his hand. "I think it happened now because you were here. When I woke up, I felt so protected. The bad thoughts from yesterday tried to work their way back in, but because you were holding us"—I rest our hands against my stomach—"they didn't find any room."

Hunter inhales sharply, his eyes round with emotion. He leans in slowly, his intent clear, before brushing his lips with mine. Morning breath be damned, I open for him and go willingly when he breaks free from my grip to haul me closer.

The kiss is heated, but with passion and fondness, not as a precursor to more. Our mouths slow, until his forehead tips to mine, breathing each other's air.

"Good morning," he says.

"A good morning it is." We stay like that for a long moment, enjoying this new place we've found together.

My stomach growls, breaking the moment. "God, for once, could my body pretend like it still belongs to me?" I roll over on my back and stretch. Hunter's eyes follow my movements. I feel it like an extra layer of fabric as the cotton of my sleep shirt rubs across my nipples, hardened by the cold air from the window unit.

"Well, it's my job to feed that body, whomever it belongs to, so I guess I better get up." He lingers for a moment longer before pushing up and out of bed. It's my turn for my eyes to meander over his body. *Fuck*, my baby daddy is hot.

He catches me staring at his ass as he turns around and smirks at me as he covers up with his shorts.

"So, what'll it be for breakfast this morning?" His head pops out of his shirt, his hair adorably mussed. "Omelet? Or maybe pancakes and fruit?"

"Yes," I say, my stomach growling again. I never regained the lost calories from yesterday, but I'm ready to make up for it now.

Hunter's grin tells me he's also thrilled my appetite is back. "All right, I'll get going. See you out there in a few?"

"Try and keep me away."

He throws me a wink before walking out of sight. I sigh, allowing myself one more moment to bask in the happiness of the morning before rolling into a seated position and getting up to get dressed.

As I walk past the dresser and catch my reflection in the mirror above it, this time, I see a strong woman. One who's growing a baby and keeping herself healthy while doing the same for it. I don't see someone who's a percentile on a chart, or worthless in other's eyes because of her weight. It's good to be back. As my body continues to change over the next several months, I'll be ready to deal with those emotions as they come. But the one thing I know? They won't be brought on by some asshole doctor who is so small-minded he probably can't memorize pi past the second decimal.

Hunter's humming to himself when I reach the kitchen, flipping an omelet in one pan and a pancake in another. Competency kink in full effect, I squeeze my legs together at the thrum that rushes through my lady parts. I wolf whistle to show my appreciation.

The grin on his face when he turns to look at me is contagious.

"How in the world did you put this together so fast?" I ask in disbelief when he puts a steaming omelet on one plate in front of me and a stack of pancakes in the middle of the table.

"While you were napping yesterday, I did some more prep. Figured if the omelet took some coercing this morning, I would have it done in a few minutes before you talked yourself out of it."

I wince at his accurate portrayal of how I reacted to food yesterday. A moan escapes as I take a bite—the cheese, herbs, and peppers hitting my tongue all at once. Hunter nods in approval before heading to the stove to make his eggs. I force myself to slow down so I don't get sick and still have some food left to eat with him.

"I've come a long way in my issues with food, but yesterday hit all my insecurities and brought them out again."

Hunter flips his omelet. "I've never experienced the need to make a doctor glad they're surrounded by medical professionals before."

I'm quiet for a moment before saying. "I think I want to file a complaint, like Jessa suggested yesterday."

He walks over to the table, somehow balancing his eggs, a bowl of fruit, and some syrup. "I'm really glad you are. I'd never force you—it's not my place to fight your battles—but how he treated you yesterday is unacceptable."

I put two pancakes on my now empty plate and drizzle syrup. "You know, if you wanted to hold my battles' hands behind their back or something, let me get a good hit in, I think that would be okay."

His smile is as big as the mega pancake left on the plate he pulls toward him. "I'll keep that in mind."

Monday morning, I get off the elevator onto the floor WUSN occupies. The bustling energy of everyone hustling to get things done between the morning news and the midday edition is a complete contrast to the rest of my weekend. After our breakfast, we snuggled on the couch and finished the movie from the night before, sans in-person strip show. The rest of the weekend was spent meandering to whatever we wanted to do next. We were relaxed, and we were together.

Now, I'm thrown back into the fray of the workday, and for the first time, I find myself not energized by it. Maybe that's the twenty-first week talking.

"Lewis."

I whirl around, recognizing the voice of Raymond Bauer, my boss, from down the hall. I stand off to the side, waiting for him to get to me.

"Been keeping an eye on the system in the Atlantic now it's hit the Gulf of Mexico?" he asks, gesturing for me to follow him to his office. You might think I'd be offended he'd ask, but I've learned this is just how Ray starts a conversation.

"Of course. I saw it hit rapid intensification status a few hours ago."

"The midday projections are here. Take that rapid intensification and keep it climbing." My phone dings as he sends them over, saving me a few seconds from loading them myself. The wind speeds have increased by sixty mph in the past twenty-four hours. At this rate . . .

"Fuck, it's headed right for Houston," I say, thinking of how some communities are still climbing out from under the hurricane that hit last year. "These pressure numbers are dropping several millibars an hour. That's . . ."

"The making of a potential Category Five," Ray finishes for me. "I want you there. I've got a spot reserved for you with a crew who knows what they're doing to keep you safe. A few other meteorologists, ex-military. You'll work together, share footage. A major change in weather reporting."

My mind scrambles. I'm still far under the recommended cut-off date for flying, but the rest of it? Being in the fray of a hurricane, in who knows what conditions? "Who's going to cover my shifts? Isn't Elizabeth out on vacation?"

"I called her and offered to cover whatever cancellation fees they encounter and add two vacation days onto what she gets back if she comes in. Weather is going to be shit in the Caribbean with this going on anyway."

"Yeah, what meteorologist books a Caribbean vacation in August?"

"Guess her fiancé did it as a surprise and she didn't want to squash their vibe." We nod in understanding. Lay people.

"Well, I mean, I have this thing later this week—"

"This is a big deal, Lewis. I need a big deal reason for you not to go." Guess scramble time is over.

"I'm pregnant."

He sits back in his chair. "Well, that's probably the biggest deal of them all."

I nod. "I'm due end of December. I planned to talk to HR soon, to get things lined up, but—"

"But you're a woman in a cutthroat field, so there's no right time to tell." My face must display my surprise because he laughs. "I have a sister, a wife, and two daughters. I know about cis, white man privilege. It's why I lobbied for you to get the job and found a way for you to do forecasts your way when the brass made me tell you to tone it down."

And here I spent all this time thinking of Ray as the bad guy. Instead, he's a really good guy who didn't want to pass the buck.

Hmm. As I reach up to wipe my eyes, I think at least he knows I'm pregnant and not fully in control of my hormones.

"Well, you can't go to Houston. Damn, I really wanted this spot . . ."

"Send Elizabeth." It's out of my mouth before I consider the potential downfall of sending the thin, beautiful Zendaya looka-like out on a major assignment in my place. I shake myself internally. Break the ceiling and reach back to pull women with you, and all that.

"You think she can do it?" Ray asks. This time I hide my surprise better. He's asking my opinion?

"Yeah, I think she's got what it takes. And I'd love for her to keep doing the online stuff while I'm out on maternity leave to keep people interested. If there's the budget, we could work together on it when I get back."

Ray nods. "A perk of you telling me you're pregnant now is I can fight to get the budget to make it happen. Now, let's brainstorm what Elizabeth needs to know to get her up to speed. I wonder if she can fly straight to Houston from St. Croix . . ."

I get home hours later, my feet each weighing one-hundred pounds. The humidity today is at an all-time high, and I'm still coming to terms with the loss of the Houston assignment. I know there's no way I could possibly take it—I huff out a laugh on the stairs imagining telling Hunter I plan to fly into a hurricane. He'd blow a gasket. But it's still disappointing to give up an opportunity like this. To gain some things, you really do have to give up others.

"Welcome home," he says, putting plates on the table as I close the front door behind me.

"You're freakishly good at that."

"I could lie, but it got done too early, so it's been warming in the oven. I pulled them out when I heard your key in the door. Careful, plate is hot."

I collapse onto the chair with more melt than normal.

"Everything okay?"

"Yeah. I mean, there's a major hurricane heading toward Texas, and I don't get to go cover it. So, I guess things aren't so great for the people in the path, but I'm okay."

"Wait, they were going to send you to cover a hurricane? Like in person? Not from a studio?" His eyes widen with each question.

"You heard where I said I'm not going, right?" I stab the fork into my food without looking at what it is. I recognize the flavors of a Tex-Mex pasta dish I've come to love and immediately regret my tone. "Sorry, I snapped. I'm the one who told my boss I couldn't go. I also had to tell him I'm pregnant, but it's going to be a cool opportunity for my coworker. I'm genuinely happy for her, while also being genuinely disappointed for myself."

With double confirmation I'm not flying into danger, Hunter starts eating. "You know, humans have the capacity to feel more than one thing at a time." He softens the sarcasm with a wink.

"Hmm. Sounds familiar, but I don't like it." I wink back.

We move on. Hunter tells me about his day. Some more testing with the app. He's getting up to take the dishes to the sink when my phone pings.

"Ha. My boss is trying to guilt me into taking the Labor Day weekend shifts. 'Be a team player while you can, Lewis.' And I thought we made a breakthrough today." I roll my eyes and put my phone face down. Hunter's stopped in the middle of drying a pan, looking at me with pure panic.

"You're going to work over Labor Day weekend? Isn't there anyone else? I mean, I know you're incredible and your job should want you on air all the time, but Labor Day?"

"What's up, Hunt?" I ask, slightly concerned he's broken.

He lets out a rush of air. "Well, this might be the record for shortest kept surprise ever."

"What are you talking about?"

"I had this idea over the weekend and found a great deal—I booked us a cruise for the long weekend. You know, a baby moon. Now, at least that I've ruined it, I don't have to figure out a creative way to get you to take Tuesday off, in addition to the days you already have."

"Oh, that's so sweet, Hunter." I'm genuinely touched he went out of his way to surprise me. I know how stressed he is about money, so never expected a big gesture like this for a baby moon. I thought about suggesting a night or two in Annapolis or something. "Where's the cruise to?"

"The Bahamas. It leaves from Baltimore, so no flights or anything. They're doing a long weekend special, skipping some of the normal ports to fit it into five days." My face twitches, and he catches it, his falling.

"Sorry, it's ironic. You're so, so sweet. And I'm really excited. My boss and I were talking today about my coworker, the one who's taking the Houston assignment? She's coming back from the Caribbean, which is a risky bet during hurricane season. Her fiancé booked it."

"Shit. I didn't think. Are the Bahamas bad too?" He looks crestfallen, so I stand and rush over to him, wrapping my arms around his waist and putting my chin on his chest.

"Sometimes. But that's what travel insurance is for."

"Oh okay." His smile, though still dimmed, returns as he wraps his arms around me too. "I did get the insurance. We get a full credit as long as we don't get on the boat and cancel an hour ahead of time."

"Very smart," I say, leaning up to press a kiss on the tip of this nose. My eyes cross watching his smile morph into something more genuine.

"So you can tell your boss your . . ." he trails off, like he started the sentence before realizing he didn't know the end of it.

"My boyfriend did good," I say, watching Hunter's eyes light up with the word boyfriend.

"That's right. Now, your boyfriend has been home for several hours, and has not had a single thought about watching last night's episode of Survivor without you, but . . ."

"God, I regret so much Preston and Jax getting you hooked on that show." He's binged it in the background when working from home after hearing Preston and Jax have a heated debate about the last season over the fourth.

"Because I then got you hooked on it?" he says, steering me to the couch.

"I'm not hooked. I can quit whenever I want," I say, shushing him as he tries to rebut during the opening.

Settling further into the coach, he kisses my temple and whispers into my skin. "Whatever you say, girlfriend."

Epistolary Interlude #2

BRANDT BROTHERS GROUP CHAT

Preston
All ready for your cruise, Hunt?

Hayden
I can't believe you booked a cruise and didn't tell any of us in time to come too.

Duncan
You're still pouting about this, Hayden? It's their baby moon. They don't need anyone else hovering around.

Even his twin.

Hayden
Even his twin?

Well, fuck. I am predictable.

Hunter
Sorry, Hay. Well, I'm not sorry. Dunc's right. It'd be weird for you to come. But I am sorry you're upset.

Duncan
He'll get over it.

Spencer
So, got everything you need? Sunblock? Sea sickness meds? Condoms?

Hayden
The fuck he need condoms for? She's not a European brown hare. She can't get pregnant twice.

Preston
That's a thing?

Spencer
See ya out of that rabbit hole in five minutes, Prez. I know he doesn't need them for that. But. You know. It's good to be safe. Just because two of you are wifed up . . .

Hunter
First, I get the safe sex talk, but second, fuck off. That's my girlfriend.

Spencer
Whoa, whoa, whoa

Duncan
Girlfriend?

Preston
That many buzzes in a row pulled me out of a Wiki-hole. When did that happen?

Hayden
Two weeks ago when he told her about the cruise.

Hunter
Thanks, Hay. And sorry, Spence. I shouldn't have snapped. Really stressed with everything that needs to happen before we leave. I'll be lucky if I have more than ten minutes to pack.

Spencer
All good. Monogamy changes everything. Plus, leaves more space in the luggage for your speedo.

Hayden
No one needs to see those blinding white thighs.

Duncan
That's the part of the Speedo visual that concerns you?

Hayden
👋 We're twins. I pretty much know what's coming.

Preston
And with that, I'm out. Have a great trip, Hunt.

Spencer
Be sure you pay respect to the sea on the way out. She's unforgiving.

Hayden
Creepy, Spence.

Duncan
Call if you need anything.

> **Hunter**
> We'll be on a floating hotel without signal and we're not getting Wi-Fi. Talk to you all next week.

JAX, MICHELLE, LAUREL, AND CHARLOTTE

Laurel
All right. Pre-cruise checklist. All packed?

> **Michelle**
> I've got muumuus and swimsuits for days. We're all set.

Laurel
What about a dress for a nice dinner?

> **Michelle**
> Oh, did you want a complete inventory of everything I packed?

Jax
Ignore whatever is about to come out of Laurel's fingers.

Laurel
It couldn't hurt.

Charlotte
I think you guys are going to have a great time. Hayden's guilt trips aren't working on Hunter, right?

Michelle
He keeps telling me he's excited we're getting the chance to go away, just the two of us. I think he's telling himself that to stave off the guilt.

Charlotte
Twins. 🙂

Laurel
Well, you'll distract him with sex then, right? I mean, you sleep in the same bed now, you've got labels . . .

Jax
Normally, I don't condone her invasive nature, but I am curious about this one.

Charlotte
If you want to share.

Laurel
She wants to.

Michelle
I don't know that I want to, but I think I need advice.

Laurel
Yes!

Jax
Here we go.

Michelle
No. No sex yet. I'm not sure why? I've sorta got this idea in my head about it being special to wait until the cruise. But now I've built it up and am freaking out.

Jax
It was crazy hot in the spring, right?

Michelle
Yeah? I mean, I think so. Have I built it up in my head?

Laurel
No, definitely not. You were way too mopey, even before the pregnancy test, for it to not have been really fucking hot.

Michelle
I guess so . . .

Laurel
Any thoughts, ladies? Does it run in the family?

Jax
And I officially withdraw my support. You made it weird.

Laurel

Charlotte
Maybe try to remove expectations. If you guys had fun before, it'll be even better because you know each other now.

Jax
And have feelings. Ugh, feelings. They do make it better.

Laurel
Plus, ya know, pregnancy hormones.

Michelle
All right, that's enough outta you.

Love you, ladies. Talk to you when we get back.

Jax
Have fun!

Charlotte
Be safe!

Laurel
Get some!

Eighteen

MICHELLE

Twenty-four weeks pregnant

"Did you know cruise ships were this big?" I say, looking up the side of the massive boat we're about to board.

"Well, I think it's perspective. We're standing right under it. And compared to the sea, it's tiny?"

"Not helpful, Hunter." I smack his chest lightly. Anyone listening in would think he's being an ass, but this is the third time we've done this since parking the car in the long-term garage fifteen minutes ago. His first two answers were more supportive. And every time . . .

"It's still over an hour to departure. We can go home." He puts his arm around my shoulder and pulls me into him.

"No, I'll be okay once we get on board and can't see the boat anymore. Nothing to compare it to size-wise then." I hope. I'm really excited to get away, but the floating boat thing is sort of freaking me out a bit. But, with lots of new things, I'm nervous until I get started and then it gets better. Cruises will be another one of those things.

"That's the spirit." Hunter lets go of my shoulder to grab our luggage and rolls it forward as the line to board inches ahead.

That's another thing I didn't realize. How long it takes to board a cruise. It's not like a train, where you can show up five minutes before and still have time for a vending machine snack. Or an airport, even if you don't have PreCheck. I'm very ready for our cabin, a bed, and a nap.

We people watch, murmuring to each other things we see from those outside our ear shot. Soon enough, it's our turn to board.

"Tickets and waivers, please?" The cruise staffer looks at us expectantly.

Hunter shows him something on his phone. "And I submitted the waivers this morning."

Waivers? I guess it makes sense we would need to sign something. I stand there and smile, not wanting to look clueless and hold anything up.

"Hmm, I don't see them marked as completed when I scanned your ticket. You'll need to—"

"Darius, Ms. Hannigan is stuck on gangway C again convinced she's going to fall in. You know you're the only one who can talk her down." A woman in her twenties joins our group. "Sorry for the interruption, folks."

Darius sighs. "I don't know why they keep letting that woman back on the boat. She causes trouble the whole trip."

"Maybe she's a con artist too," I say. Hunter looks at me curiously, and Darius and the new woman give me blank stares. "You know, Mrs. Hannigan? Annie? The musical? Jamie Foxx did a remake, but the one from the '80s is way better . . ." Still nothing. "Isn't there a woman in distress somewhere?" Better to take my losses.

Darius takes off without another word, and the woman looks at us. "Enjoy your trip, y'all. Make sure you sign up for the shuffleboard tournament. Hear it's a hoot."

She turns to the next people in line to scan their tickets. Hunter snorts beside me.

"Oh, you think that's funny, huh? Just because I quote a movie from the '80s doesn't mean I want to enter a shuffleboard tournament." We move onto the boat and follow directions toward our room.

"I know, babe. But let me know if I should move our dinner reservations earlier before we lose cell service, okay?" His shoulders are shaking with laughter.

"See if I put sunscreen on your back at all, mister." Hunter laughs in earnest. "Keep on walking." I push him ahead of me, smiling so he knows I'm not mad.

We find our room a short time later. It's cozy, but I expected it to be. Hunter mentioned looking into an upgrade last week, but I shut him down. I'm okay with cozy.

Hunter tucks our luggage out of the way as I flop onto the bed, sending the swan towels flying before rolling onto my side. I might regret not bringing the new pregnancy pillow I finally caved and bought a couple weeks ago, but I worried about there being enough room for me, the pillow, and Hunter on the bed. Hunter said I could use him as a pillow instead.

"Ready for a nap before pinochle, Mich?" His jab loses its edge when he sits on the bed next to me, running his fingers through my hair in the way he knows relaxes me.

"I am ready for a nap. Thank you very much. And besides, didn't anyone ever tell you to respect your elders?" I don't bother to open my eyes, letting his fingers and the slight rocking of the boat lull me toward relaxation.

"Some of my thoughts for later are anything but respectful." His lips ghost along the shell of my ear as he talks, voice husky and low. My eyes fly open and heat runs through me.

By the time I get myself rolled over and propped up, he's standing at the door, eyes mischievous and tracing over me.

"You're going to use that voice and leave?"

He laughs, still using the low tenor of his range. "We're still at port, babe. Plus, I think you're going to need that nap. I'm going to go get the lay of the land and let you sleep. I'll be back." He blows me a kiss and slips out the door.

I throw my limbs down on the mattress and let out a gust of breath. Guess maybe I'm not the only one who thought a cruise might be a good place for sex. Well game on, Brandt. I steal a pillow from his side of the bed and arrange it under my hip to give me a bit more support and lay back down. A quick nap, and then I'll be ready.

"Michelle. Babe. Dinner's in thirty minutes. It's time to get up."

My eyes slowly open before the meaning of his words kick in. "Thirty minutes?! That means it's . . ." I try to remember what time Hunter said dinner was tonight.

"It's six thirty. Dinner's at seven." Hunter's lying next to me, dress pants on, but shirtless.

"This is a look." I nod at all the ink on display.

He laughs. "I didn't want to wrinkle my shirt, but wanted to watch you sleep for a bit."

"You do it every day. You're always awake before me." I try to hide it in my tone, but I actually love his blue eyes being one of the first things I see every day now. Hunter never went back to his bed after the first sleepover a few weeks ago.

The soft smile on his face tells me he sees right through me. "Plus, I tried to wake you up earlier, and you were having none of it."

I do remember telling him five more minutes. The light is lower, so it must have been a while ago.

"Okay, well, good thing all my dresses are low maintenance and sea water makes the waves extra wavy." I gesture to my hair, hoping I'll be able to salvage it since there's no time to shower.

"You're beautiful," he says, pressing a kiss to the tip of my nose before pushing himself up. That's sweet and all, but where's the disrespectful guy from before?

He holds out a hand to help me sit up. "Besides. Every minute we're late for dinner is another minute I'll make you wait before I let you come."

There he is.

"I'm not sure if that makes me want to hurry up or slow down," I say, reaching out to trace down Hunter's chest. He tries to move out of my reach, but the small quarters close him in, and he ends up thrusting his crotch toward me. My hand grazes a semi-hard cock before he manages to pull that away too. I raise an eyebrow at him.

"Dinner. Star gazing on the upper deck. Then you can touch all you want."

I shove off the bed and head into the tiny bathroom.

"Unless we're late."

I look over my shoulder. "Promises, promises," I say, before shutting the bathroom door.

Try as I might, I can't convince Hunter to skip the star gazing portion of the evening. His hand inched up my thigh all through dinner. Higher and higher until his fingertips grazed my mound, and then he'd remove it to take a sip of the one glass of wine he nursed all dinner before starting the path again at my knee. My underwear would be soaked—if I were wearing any. Thank God for light, patterned fabric.

Hunter leads me to the railing at the far end of the deck, bracketing me with his arms. His front presses in against my back. "Five minutes," he says into my ear, and I let out a frustrated breath, knowing I'm not going to win my quest to shorten this part of the evening. We stand there for a moment as our eyes adjust to the lower light on this part of the ship. The next time I look up, there are stars everywhere. So many stars, like I've never seen before.

I must make a noise, because Hunter runs his nose down the back of my ear before saying, "Told you." He retreats into silence as we stand there, taking in the expanse of the sky afforded by pitch darkness out at sea.

"Five minutes is up," he says after what could have been thirty seconds or two hours.

"Maybe five more." A breeze brushes across the deck and I shiver. Hunter gathers me closer and rests his chin on top of my head. For a moment, we're the only two people on the planet and I'm glad he's the only other one. I'll have to remember to tell him later I'm glad he didn't let me skip this.

The breeze picks up and cuts right through my thin dress. Hunter's heat is doing its best to fight it, but my shivering picks up.

"C'mon. We can come back up tomorrow night. We'll bring more layers." He holds out his hand and laces our fingers together as we walk to the cabin.

Given my eagerness to skip to this part of the evening earlier, I'm surprised to find my stomach full of butterflies as we make our way down the final hallway before it's just the two of us. Behind a closed door. With every intention of having sex.

Once we're in our closet of a room, the butterflies have had babies and multiplied. Hunter flashes me a knowing smile. "C'mere," he says, opening his arms. I walk right into them. Inhaling his cedar scent, his arms wrap around me, the kiss he presses to the top of my head, every worry I had calms. This is Hunter, the one who made me come alive in the bedroom in a way no one ever has. And we didn't even know each other then.

He opens his mouth, presumably to tell me there's no pressure. I cover his lips with my hand, cutting him off, before pulling his head down, replacing my hand with my lips. My tongue traces the seam of his mouth, asking for entry as my hands clutch at his broad, strong shoulders.

He groans as he opens for me, his hands moving down to my ass, pulling me as tightly to him as he can with my pregnant belly between us. His fingers curve, cupping a cheek in each hand as our mouths move against each other, tongues dancing.

"Where's your underwear, baby?" He mutters against my lips.

"Looks like I left it in the suitcase," I say, speaking the words against his skin, kissing my way down his neck.

He growls, pulling my dress up my legs until he can slip his hands under fabric. One circles back to resume its grip on my ass, while the other seeks my center. I widen my legs slightly to let his fingers slide through where I'm slick, inviting him in.

With his mouth on my ear, he says, "All this wetness, one layer away all night. It's a good thing I didn't know, or I may have dropped under the tablecloth and had you for dinner." His fingers sweep across my clit, once, twice before he brings his hand from under my dress. Leaning back, he brings his fingers to his lips and tastes me on it. "Even sweeter than I remember."

A shudder racks through my body and I step back before I get too lost in the moment. His hands follow, reaching for me, but he lets me take my space.

"Hold that thought. I'm going to go freshen up and slip into something more comfortable." I snag a black bundle from my bag and walk to the bathroom, taking a peek over my shoulder. Hunter looks wrecked, his lips swollen and red, hair standing up from my hands running through it.

"As long as you promise not to add any underwear," he says as I reach the door to the bathroom.

"As long as I come out here to find you in only your underwear, you've got yourself a deal." Hunter's fingers immediately start working on the buttons on his shirt.

Alone in the bathroom, I catch myself in the mirror, my lips as well used as Hunter's, with a hint of red on my cheeks from his stubble. The anxious woman from before is long gone.

After I freshen up, I slip the long dress over my head and replace it with a sheer black nighty. It's no green lace bodysuit, but the silkiness of the fabric lights up my nerve endings. Deciding there's no reason to hide how bad I want it. I rush out to the bedroom. The sight of Hunter stops me short. Lying on the bed, he did as I asked and removed all his clothes except for his boxer briefs. What I didn't expect was for him to pull his cock out above the waist band, leisurely stroking it up and down while waiting for me.

"Starting without me?" I ask, lifting an eyebrow.

"I wouldn't dream of it," he says, his eyes roving over my body, taking in the way the fabric skims the top of my thighs and the sheer fabric allows the rose color of my nipples to show through. "Fuck, Michelle. You look . . . Well, your tits—"

"Look insane, right?" I cut him off, both of us grinning at the echo from our night together in March. Little did we know they'd look even more insane thanks to a little Cumulus growing inside me.

"Get over here so I can taste them," he says, his voice pulling me to him like a magnet. I climb up on the bed and straddle his lap. His cock lays forgotten against his stomach, still above the waistband of his briefs. We both hiss as my bare skin meets the hard thickness. Hunter digs his hands into my hips, pulling them back slightly as he bends to take one of my nipples into his mouth. The stinging bite, following by soothing licks, sends a bolt of heat to my pussy, and my hips rock up on their own, seeking friction. My clit glides along his cock, and I groan as I continue to rock back and forth, overwhelmed by the sensation at my breasts and the bundle of nerves at my core.

Another groan vibrates from Hunter's chest, this one vibrating against the nipple he's tending through the fabric. His hands help guide me along his cock before squeezing tight and holding me still. His eyes clamp shut, and he breathes deep, searching for his control. When they open, they find mine immediately, and my breath catches at the hunger I see in them.

"I wanted to take this slow, make it last, but if I don't get inside your cunt in the next few seconds, I might die."

Not wanting my pussy to be responsible for any deaths, I reach between us and with his help work his underwear further down his thighs before he manages to kick them off. Gripping his cock tight in my fist, I move my hand up and down once before holding it up and lowering myself onto him.

"Fuck, Clyde. Michelle," Hunter groans against my shoulder as he inches into my tightness. "You feel so good bare around my dick." I start to lift my hips, following the urge to move, but he tightens his grip once more. "You're going to need to give me a minute."

He tilts his head back, eyes closed. I lean forward to graze his lips. One hand leaves my side to tangle in my hair, tilting my head right where he wants it. "Baby, I'm going to need you to move," I mutter against his mouth, feeling I might come apart at the seams if he doesn't.

"Anything for you," he answers as the hand at my hips guides me upward before his hips piston up, thrusting deeper than before.

"Fuck yes," I say, using my knees to meet his tempo. "Just like that." Sweat breaks out on my brow, a drop running down my back under the fabric that suddenly feels restrictive instead of luxurious.

Like he's reading my mind, Hunter pulls the offending garment up over my head and throws it to the side. His mouth latches immediately to my bare breast, biting down hard enough to leave a mark on the underside. My channel constricts in time with the pain and his gasp heats against my skin.

"Harder, please," I manage to ask, even as my rhythm falters. Hunter takes over, moving me up and down on his cock, plunging hard and deep with each thrust. I lean back slightly, changing the angle, and then he's hitting that spot every time.

"Yes, right there."

Through gritted teeth, he says, "I'm going to need you to get there, Michelle. Can you come for me?"

Like my body was simply waiting for him to ask, I shatter, yelling out.

"Beautiful," Hunter mutters, before pounding up once, twice, more before holding me tightly on his cock. It's my turn to open my eyes as his warmth fills me, unable to look away from this man falling off the cliff into his orgasm. The visual and the pulses inside me spur an aftershock to run through my body.

No longer able to hold my body upright, I collapse forward onto Hunter's chest, pushing him against the headboard. We stay like that, sweat cooling on our bodies as our breathing slows. All the while, Hunter's hand strokes up and down my back.

After a while, Hunter softens enough he slips out of me, and I wince as the gush of liquid spills onto the bed.

"Don't worry," he says, pushing his lips against my temple. "I'll sleep in the wet spot." He helps me off his lap and onto my side. "I'll be right back," he says, slipping off to the bathroom. My eyes stay closed longer and longer with each blink, and I'm asleep before Hunter returns.

CHAPTER
Nineteen

HUNTER

Twenty-four weeks pregnant

I wake up to a wet heat enveloping my cock. A tongue runs up from root to tip before sucking the head into her mouth. My hips thrust up once, waking me the rest of the way up. The sight of Michelle straddling my legs with my dick in her mouth, her tits bouncing as she moves up and down my shaft, awaits me. My hand finds its way into her hair, not putting any pressure on her head, but wanting to feel her head move as she takes me as deep as she can.

Wanting to try something, I tug on the fistful of hair I'm entwined in and am rewarded with a groan vibrating the whole way to my balls. She brings me to her lips, almost letting me fall from her mouth, when she drags her teeth along a spot at the bottom of my cockhead. I reward her for the effort with another hip thrust. The resulting smile tells me that's the response she was looking for. Suddenly, my orgasm is right around the corner.

"Mich, if you don't stop, I'm going to come," I say, releasing her hair, expecting her to pull off. Instead, she takes me to the back of her throat, swallowing around the tip. That's it for me and I'm coming down her throat. My toes curl and it's an effort to fight the instinct to plant my legs as my soul empties into her via my dick. She swallows every drop and licks me clean until I'm too sensitive.

"Holy fuck," I breathe out between chest heaving inhales. My spit covered cock falls against my stomach as she sits up. "Where did that come from?"

"A perk of fighting my gag reflex so often," she says, a smug expression on her face, settling on the mattress, her legs crossed in front of her.

"Who knew?" My breaths slow, energy starting to return. "How wet did sucking me off make you?" I ask, pushing myself into a sitting position.

"Why don't you get over here and find out," she sasses.

"Oh, I intend to do much more than that." I climb out of bed, answering her puzzled look by gripping a shin in each hand and unfolding her legs. Once they're untangled from each other, I give each foot a good yank, pulling her toward me and the edge of the bed. My fingers dip into her pussy, coming back glistening. "So wet. Someone likes sucking my cock, don't they?"

She nods, proud of how much she enjoys giving me pleasure. Luckily, that's an interest we share.

Reaching up alongside her body, I trace a path up her stomach to the valley between her breasts with my tongue. "I'm going to need to fuck these tits before Cumulus arrives," I say against her skin. Her breath catches, telling me she's on board with the idea.

"But for now . . ." I trail off, gripping two pillows in my hand and dragging them toward the edge of the bed while I retrace my course down her body. I drop one pillow on the ground and kneel on it. "Lift up." I direct, patting her half on the hip, half on the side of her ass cheek. She complies and I tuck the second pillow under the lower back. "I don't want you getting stiff, because I intend to stay down here for a long while."

With that, I push her thighs apart, taking in her slick, pink center. She moans and takes her breasts in her hands. "I feel your eyes like a feather, whispering over where I want you. Touch me, please."

"How can I resist a direct invitation?" I lean forward, licking from her center to her clit. I stay at that bundle of nerves, flicking it from side to side with my tongue before sucking it into my mouth. Her hips cant up, letting me know what's burned in my memory is accurate. I continue focusing on her clit while coating two fingers in her wetness before pushing inside her. Another groan emits from her throat, so I pick up the pace with both my mouth and my hand, curling my fingers to hit the spongey spot along her inner wall. She tightens around my fingers and continue working my tongue along her clit through her orgasm.

I know she still has more waves to go when she tries to squeeze her legs closed. "I don't think so," I say. "I'm not done with you yet." I lift each leg, so they're hooked over my shoulders, forcing her legs to stay open. She moans but doesn't protest. I lean back toward her core. Taking time to press kisses up and down the skin on her inner thigh, right to the edge of her lips, wanting to give her time to recover slightly. In what seems like no time at all, she's shifting her hips, trying to force my tongue more central. Her being so hungry for my mouth takes my recovering cock from half-hard to stiff against my thigh. He'll need to wait his turn.

I give her what I'm looking for, fucking her with my tongue for a few thrusts before moving to her clit. Using her wetness on my fingers again, I trail them down toward her crease, tapping lightly against her puckered hole. She stills for a moment before circling her hips, inviting my light exploration of her backdoor.

"Have you ever had anything here?" I say into her pussy, as I continue my gentle touching, not wanting to lose contact with my favorite taste for longer than I need to.

"No-o," she shudders out, her hips thrusting. I stiffen my

tongue, allowing her to use me to take what she needs against her clit.

"Someday, I'd love to take you here," I say. "But we'll work up to that." She continues to ride my face and a new gush of liquid along with her noises lets me know she's crested again. Her knees try to squeeze shut, and I'd gladly blackout with her thighs as my new favorite ear muffs any other day, but it might put a damper on the trip.

Michelle's legs go limp, and I look up her body to see her looking down at me from her elbows, her face visible above the baby bump that's more pronounced with her clothes off.

"Can you take another one?" I ask, continuing to lick as she shudders against me.

"No, please. Want you inside me."

That's a request I'll always be happy to oblige. I press a kiss to the top of her mound before letting her legs down from my shoulders, leaving them dangling over the edge of the bed.

I climb up over her body, and she pulls my face down to hers, tasting herself on my mouth. Once our lips slow, I pull back slightly. "I want to hold you and fuck you nice and slow."

She nods, words seeming beyond her two orgasms in. I pull the pillow from under her hip and slide her up the bed before turning her onto her side. My body slots in behind hers, and I lift her leg so it rests on top of my hip. I guide myself into her channel, groaning as I slide home. My hand grips under her belly and I start to thrust my hips in and out, nice and slow.

"This is how you deserve to be ma . . ." I catch myself. This feels a lot like making love to me, but I know enough to not drop that bomb during sex. "Deserve to be fucked. Slow, like you're precious. Because you are. You're so precious to me."

Her fingers intertwine with mine on her stomach, gripping tightly as she turns her head, searching for my mouth. I push up to meet her, tangling our tongues for a moment until she groans with a swivel of my hips and drops her cheek to the pillow. I stay propped up, trailing kisses from her ear, along her neck, and to her shoulder. All the while, my hips pump in and out of her, adding a circular thrust every few joinings.

After a while, Michelle starts to press her hips back into mine, trying to speed up the pace. I oblige and untangle our fingers, bringing my hand to her clit. Strumming along the bud for a few seconds in time with our thrusts has her tightening around me once more, her mouth open in a silent scream. I follow her over the edge, my not silent groan pressed into her skin.

We stay connected like that, long enough I think she's fallen asleep. I know I should roll away and get a cloth to clean us up, but I'm reluctant to lose the contact.

Just as I've talked myself into moving, Michelle breaks the silence.

"Hunter?" she says, her voice quiet and tired, but content.

"Yeah," I respond, pressing another kiss into her shoulder.

"You deserve to be fucked like that too."

I'm stunned. My arm wraps tighter around her and I bury my face in her neck. Cleaning up can wait.

Turns out, the way the ocean lets you see stars forever also means there's nothing to block the sunlight once it's over the horizon. The light through our small port window brightens the room as I try to catch the time on my phone without moving Michelle. Not even six a.m.

I look up at the curtain we didn't bother to draw and down at the woman using my legs and my pillows to prop herself up. When we finally called it quits a few hours ago, she had a hard time getting comfortable. A crick in my neck from using my arm as a pillow is nothing compared to what her body is going through. Though, maybe I can snag an extra or two off a housekeeper today.

I don't think I can move to cover the window without

waking her up. If she needed a three-hour nap to recover from boarding a boat, she'll definitely need more than a handful of hours to make it through a full day. The beam of light inches up our bodies, moving toward our heads. That settles it. I move one limb at a time very slowly. Michelle readjusts but doesn't seem to wake. I roll off the bed as gently as I can, scooch around the bed and have moved the curtain into place when . . .

"What time is it?"

Fuck. "It's a little after six."

She groans. "Why is it so bright out?"

"All that wide-open space. No trees, no buildings, no hills to block the light."

"Gross. All this light is making me sick."

I laugh. "You may have a hickey or two, but I don't think I turned you—"

"Wait." She sits up. "No, I think I'm really going to be sick."

"Fuck." That one is out loud. I grab the trash can and hand it to her. "Do you want to try to make it to the bathroom?"

She nods, and I notice how pale she is. I got too caught up in worrying about the sunlight and how right she felt against me to pick up on it earlier. Each of us holding one side of the trash can, we get her standing and move the few feet into the bathroom. Never more thankful for tight quarters, we make it to the toilet in time for Michelle to let loose into the bowl.

"Yuck, it's like it's week eleven all over again." She heaves into the toilet once more. Looking around, wanting to be helpful, I pull a washcloth off the shelf and wet it with cold water. I hand it to her, along with some tissue for around her mouth.

She leans against the wall. "Do you mind grabbing me a pillow? We can get a replacement from housekeeping later, but this is going to kill my back sitting on the floor."

It sounds like we're in it for the long haul. I rush into the bedroom and grab one of the pillows she had at her hips. The sound of Michelle retching again reaches my ears. I look at the bed and grab the whole damn comforter off. If she's going to be on the floor in a cruise ship bathroom, it's going to be the most comfortable floor I can give her.

I lean against the wall as she goes another few rounds. She leans back into the nest I made her and wipes her hand across her head. I rewet the washcloth and hand it to her.

"Thanks. Shit, have you used the bathroom this morning? I think all the liquid that can be expelled from my body has come out my mouth, but . . ."

My bodily functions had been entirely forgotten, but now that she mentions it, I really do need to piss.

"Uh, maybe I can run up and use the one in the locker room." I calculate how long it will take me to get there and back, and if I can risk leaving her for that long.

"Hunter. My man. Your dick has impregnated me and been inside me within the last six hours. I think you can piss with me in the same room. Promise I won't look." She turns her head to the side and holds her hand over her eyes.

It's tricky to maneuver, but I get close enough to the toilet. It takes a second, but things start flowing. "You can't cover both your eyes and your ears at the same time. You don't have the hands." I mutter, the tips of my ears growing warm.

The flush and rush of water from the sink lets her know it's okay to remove her hand, and she looks at me. Her face betrays her exhaustion, but she tries to give me her best smile, anyway. "All new levels of intimacy reached this weekend." She holds out her hand for a high five, but instead I grab it and hang on, sliding down the wall to sit next to her. She leans her shoulder against me, and we wait.

A couple hours later, the heaving has slowed way down, but now, I'm worried about rehydrating her. This much vomit is dangerous enough when it's just you, but with the baby, it's a lot worse.

"Do you think you can try some water?" I ask. I'd really love to get some food in her too, but one step at a time. She puts on a brave face as I hand her a newly filled glass, and she takes a small sip.

"Take it slow," I say, holding my breath. She nods, then takes another sip. Then one more. She sets the glass down hard, spilling water on the floor and the comforter as she leans over the toilet again.

"What is wrong with me?" Her eyes fill and spill over. From exhaustion, fear, or plain feeling awful, I'm not sure. I sit down on the wet ground and rub her back.

"The boat does seem to be a bit rockier today," I say. "The water might have changed. Or maybe it's something you ate last night?"

"You had the same thing I did, and you're fine."

At this point, I'm less concerned about the cause and more worried about what we do now. "I think we might need to go to the infirmary. We need to get some fluids in you." She doesn't put up an argument, which is when I decide to call and ask for a wheelchair to get her there.

Less than ten minutes later, Michelle's on an exam table and the physician's assistant who helped get us there is preparing an IV. The tight band pinched around my chest for the last few hours loosens a notch or two.

"All right, standard stuff. This happens a lot on the first full day. Any chance you came in contact with spoiled meat or produce, any history of sea sickness, any chance you might be pregnant?"

"Oh, um, yes," Michelle says. The PA stops in their tracks.

"Which one is that yes for?" It's clear most of the time the answer is no.

"I'm pregnant," Michelle says slowly.

The PA looks at me and looks back at Michelle. "You can't tell?" I ask. I've been able to pick out Michelle's baby bump for weeks now, but I guess if you didn't know her, because of her shape, you might not know.

"Hey, now. I assume no one's pregnant until they tell me or

have a baby." The PA holds up their hands for a second, then gets back to work setting the IV. "How far along are you?"

"Twenty-four weeks," she says, hissing as the needle goes in.

"Fuck, sorry." They pause for a second, then connect the line to the port he just put into her hand. "You guys signed the waivers, right?"

"Is something wrong with the IV? Her vein?" I stand up to look.

"Oh, no. I mean, she did surprise me with her answer, but no damage done. A bit more of a pinch than there should have been, I'm sorry. I mean, the waiver saying you weren't boarding the boat past twenty-three weeks pregnant."

I sit back down. Fuck. I skimmed through the waivers before I signed them, but never thought to check about any pregnancy restrictions. She can fly until thirty-six weeks, maybe a little less if her blood pressure rises. Why would this be any different?

"Why is that the rule? I can fly for another twelve weeks."

"Because unlike an airplane, we can't make an emergency landing if something goes wrong." A sharp voice filters in from the entrance to the infirmary.

CHAPTER
Twenty

HUNTER

Twenty-four weeks pregnant

"Dr. Patricia Gibson. I'm the ship's doctor. So. You decided you could ignore the line in the waiver about the pregnancy limit and cross your fingers nothing bad happened?" She pinches the skin on Michelle's hand to watch how long it takes to fall back into place. "This looks like dehydration. Probably didn't drink enough water when boarding yesterday. With the proneness toward nausea, the choppier surf today sealed your fate."

She turns her eyes on both Michelle and me in turn. Michelle looks at me too. She didn't call me on the waiver thing yesterday, but I know it's my fuck-up to speak up for now. "This probably isn't much better than disregarding it, but we . . . I didn't see the clause. I signed for both of us. We only booked a few weeks ago. This is the only time we can get away. Things with work were so busy, and I forgot about the waivers and signed them without looking for anything about pregnancy. My assumption was along the flying timeline too. I'd . . ." My voice catches, and Michelle grabs my hand and squeezes it once. It's a reassurance I don't deserve. "I'd never knowingly put her in danger. Please, is she going to be okay?" I look searchingly at Dr. Gibson and the PA. The doctor's face morphs into something slightly more sympathetic. "We're going to keep her in here until we anchor later this afternoon and keep an eye on her levels. If it's simply dehydration, like I assume it is, she's going to be just fine with rest and more fluids."

The band around my chest loosens another notch. "Thank you." The rest of what she said replays in my head. "Wait, anchor this afternoon? The first port isn't until tomorrow morning, right?"

The sympathy leaves Dr. Gibson's face and is replaced by something more stoic, like you would find on a general who has to give orders to her troops she disagrees with. "The cruise line's policy is if you're more than twenty-three weeks pregnant while on board, we have to remove you at the next viable port option. That's Eleuthera. They have a small clinic and planes come in and out of the airport a few times a week. It's been a while since I last looked at their schedule, but they usually have a small charter departing on Saturday afternoons. We might make it in time."

Michelle's mouth opens in shock. "You just . . . leave us there?"

"I am sorry, Ms. Lewis. It's for your own safety."

I want to rage there's nothing safe about leaving a pregnant woman on an island without a guaranteed way off and a "small clinic." The urge to upend the neatly organized medical supplies on the shelf along the wall across from me simmers underneath my skin. But I've already caused enough trouble. I won't make this any worse for us.

"We understand," I say. Michelle whips her head in my direction in shock.

Dr. Gibson presses a button. "Bill, do you want to help Mr. Brandt pack up their cabin? I'll stay with Ms. Lewis."

"Yes, ma'am." A porter steps through the doorway from who the fuck knows where. I stand up to follow him, dropping Michelle's hand. I follow Bill out without looking back. The band around my chest is tighter than ever, threatening to cut off my oxygen. Only a handful of hours ago, I woke up, having everything I never knew I wanted in my arms. And now, I've risked them. For what? To play the romantic? The guy who woos the girl? That's not my role.

Hours later, Michelle's coloring is much better. I force myself to meet her eyes as they get us on a smaller boat to make our way to Eleuthera. All the sparkle, the shimmer that matched the stars we watched last night, has disappeared. I snuffed it out.

I instead watch the people standing on their balconies and against the railing, watching us leave them behind. Michelle leans into my side then, and I tuck her under my arm. Not because I deserve to be her shelter, but because no one should think she did anything to get us this treatment. It's all on me.

The crew member who brought us over makes sure we flag down a rickshaw pulled by a bike before taking off. The driver straps our luggage in.

"Airport?" he asks. It seems like this isn't the first time two people have arrived on his island off a large boat like this.

"Yes, please," Michelle says. He starts pedaling and turns up a radio, the sound carrying on the wind as we move away from the shore.

"Hunter." She touches my arm. "This isn't your fault."

Despite my best intentions, I'm not able to hold back my scoff. "How is this not my fault? First, I didn't consider hurricane season when I booked, but luck and weather patterns bailed me out of that one. I didn't tell you there was a waiver. I forged your signature. Fuck, I'm pretty sure you should sue me. Duncan can find you a lawyer."

Saying Duncan's name brings forward the thought I've been trying to bat away all afternoon. One call to Duncan will solve all this. But I'll also have to admit to my oldest brother I fucked up and need him to save me. *Again*.

Michelle sits up straighter, prepared to argue with me. "I could have researched what I needed to know about going on a cruise pregnant. I mean, I did look things up, but not that part. What sunscreen can I wear? Pregnancy sea sickness prevention methods. Remember, it took two of us to board the boat. You're not alone in this." She repeats a variation on the words I said to her weeks ago, but they don't penetrate the buzzing in my head.

A buzzing sound outside my head grows louder, and I watch as a plane takes off from behind the buildings in front of us and into the sky. It grows smaller and smaller as it gains height and distance.

"There must be a chance of weather between here and the mainland," our driver calls over his shoulder. "Sometimes they run ahead of schedule if they have everything they know they're waiting on. There's another plane on Wednesday. I can take you to the airport to check on space and then get you somewhere to stay for a couple days."

"Wednesday. Shit. There must be Wi-Fi here, right? If they have an airport? I'll have to email Ray. We scheduled a meeting to talk about the schedule for our fall foliage predictions and coverage when I got back on Wednesday."

And now I'm affecting her job? Another fault I can add to the list.

We pull up in front of a small airport. Michelle walks toward the door, but I grab the driver's shoulder. "We, uh, might not need a place to stay the whole way until the next scheduled flight. Private planes can land here?" The driver nods. "Okay, I need to make a call, but hopefully we'll be out of here tomorrow or the day after. Let me know how much I owe you too. I don't have a ton of cash, but I can have money wired too."

There's something like sympathy in his gaze. "The cruise line provides for these types of situations. It's handled. I'll go make sure your woman is all right. You make your call. It's all going to be all right, son."

I nod, my throat tight. I don't know how he can be so sure.

I pull out my phone and am thankful to see a single bar. Saves me from asking for a Wi-Fi password, or worse, asking to use someone else's phone. I'd rather not be overheard.

"Brandt Investing International, Mr. Brandt's office. How can I help you?"

I hate when he forwards his cell to his assistant. I clear my throat. "Uh, hi. This is Hunter. Is Duncan around?"

"Mr. Brandt has a very full schedule today." I roll my eyes. It's Saturday of a three-day weekend. Get a life, bro. "May I ask what this is in regard to?"

My patience snaps. "No, you may fucking not. Can you please put my brother on the phone?"

My outburst is met with silence before a shaky voice says. "One moment please," and I'm met with staticky muzak. Fuck, I'm going to hear about that one.

"Hunter. Didn't expect to hear from you, especially not from an assistant near tears. Making them cry is my job. What's up?"

I can't bring myself to say anything.

"Hunter, you there?" Duncan's voice changes, dropping all the ritz that's crept in over the years of his success. What's left is my big brother. "Is everything okay?"

"You knew I'd fuck this up, didn't you? That's why you told me to call if I needed something?" My voice cracks, and I hear the tears in my words, matching the ones rolling down my cheeks.

"What? No." It's the first time in a long time I've heard him sound bewildered. "I say it to all of you whenever you leave the country, just in case. But I guess . . ."

"I've never left the country before. Barely done fucking anything worth remembering before."

"Hunter . . ."

"I can't right now. We're on Eleuthera. The cruise line has a policy against passengers being over twenty-three weeks pregnant onboard. Michelle got dehydrated and sick, so they found out she's past their policy limit and dropped us off in the next viable place." I rush through the words, hoping if I get them out quick, it won't sound as awful. It doesn't work.

"Fuck, they just drop you off? That doesn't sound legal."

"It is. It's in the waiver I signed without reading." It's a sign Duncan knows how upset I am he doesn't interject there. "The next plane isn't until Wednesday. The doctor on the boat says she's fine after some IVs, but after how sick she was this morning, I want Michelle off this island as soon as possible. Can you . . . can you help?"

"Parker." I hear Duncan yell for his assistant instead of wasting time answering me. "I need you to get a private plane chartered to Eleuthera. One of our standard pilots, double their fee to dump any existing flights. Tonight, if they can, first thing tomorrow, if not." I hear Parker agree in the affirmative, not that he has any choice, before Duncan directs his attention back to me.

"I've got you, Hunt. Do you want a nurse on the flight too to check Michelle? You know what? Fuck it. We're doing it. I'm going to work on getting someone myself while Parker gets the flight. I'll send you the information once we have it."

I nod, forgetting he can't see me. But he must sense my agreement.

"I'd do anything for you, Hunt. Please never forget that. Let's fix it now, and talk it through later, okay? Love you."

He's gone before I can respond. "Thanks. Love you too," I say to the empty line.

I stand in the warm sun, taking a few deep breaths. In other circumstances, I might find this place to be paradise. I'll never know.

Wiping my face, I head inside to update Michelle and wait for someone else to save my ass. Again.

CHAPTER
Twenty-One

MICHELLE

Twenty-six weeks pregnant

The past two weeks have been some of the longest of my life. The weeks between learning I was pregnant and finding Hunter again? The blink of an eye compared to the weeks since we got home from the cruise.

Duncan had a jet land at dawn the next morning. I slept on a couch in the airport while Hunter sat in a chair next to me. The bags under his eyes made me think he didn't sleep at all.

That's when the silence started.

It continued as the nurse on board the private jet started a thorough exam as soon as we were at cruising altitude. Hunter's eyes watched intently as she billed me in good health, and then promptly handed me an electrolyte drink. I smiled at him as I sipped it like a good little patient. He nodded and looked out the window.

After we got home, he made some excuses about not wanting to disturb me while I slept—me needing my rest and wanting to be sure I had enough room for my pillow. He started sleeping in his room that night and hasn't entered my bedroom since.

I sit, watching as my "boyfriend" does the dishes after another dinner he made for me. It probably tasted delicious, but I stayed too busy trying to force a conversation to tell. Sure, he asks how my day went and doesn't ignore a direct question, but that's it. The banter, the fire, the laughter. It's gone out.

I excuse myself to take a long bath. It's the most excitement Hunter's shown in a few days. I'm not sure if it's the fact I'm doing something for myself or I'll be occupied for at least an hour that's lighting him up. Regardless, I feel like my muscles are going to knot up so much I'll gain weird bumps on my shoulders like body builders have if I don't do something to try to relax. The last of the bubble bath Hunter pretended to find for me at a grocery store spills under the roaring faucet. Fitting. I slip under the bubbles and breathe in deep, trying to let the lavender and eucalyptus scent relax me. Instead, my mind quiets enough to hear my mother's voice.

"Don't get knocked up to keep a man. You'll think you're tying them tighter, but they're waiting for you to open the cage so they can bolt. You need to give a man a long leash. Then he'll come back to the one who feeds him."

I dunk my head under the water, like it can wash away the thoughts from my brain. I think I was fourteen when she told me that pearl of wisdom. I came home, excited to let her know Petey Garfield asked me to homecoming. I didn't talk to her much about guys and dating afterward. She didn't return the favor.

You didn't trap him. He wanted *to be here. He's just working through some stuff. You need to give him time.*

When Hunter didn't follow me into the airport on Eleuthera, I went outside to find him. Once I realized he had called Duncan, I should have gone back inside. The pain in his voice when he said, "You knew I'd fuck this up, didn't you?" rooted me to my spot.

Trying to tell him it's not his fault hasn't worked. I tried different variations in the first few days after we got home. "I'm completely fine" was met with "but what if you weren't." And "it'll be a story to laugh about one day" actually made him leave the room. I stopped trying to assuage his guilt. He seems to want to sit with it.

I've avoided seeing any of the girls, because they'll take one look at my face and the whole thing will spill out. As far as they know, we got home on Tuesday as planned. Considering Jax hasn't broken down my door means Duncan hasn't told any of the brothers either.

I know I should make him talk about things. But every time I try to get the courage to bring it up, my mother's voice rings again. *"Don't be a nag. Maybe if you waited on him for a change."*

"No," I say out loud, bringing my hands down onto the water, sending some of it cascading over the side of the tub. That's going to be a bitch to clean up.

"Michelle? You okay? I heard you say something and then a big splash?"

How the hell did he hear me? I open my mouth to say everything's fine, but eye the water on the floor and my robe hanging on the back of the door. Instead, I say, "I'm okay. But I slipped a little trying to get up. Can you come help me?"

The door is open in another second, Hunter's eyes tracing over my body in the tub, as if he needs to see for himself I really am okay. I start to regret tricking him when I see his eyes linger, his brain releasing the worry of me being hurt and processing my nakedness instead. He shakes himself.

"Yeah, of course. Let me . . ." he trails off, frozen between grabbing my robe first or getting me up. He finally grabs the robe off the hook, lays it across the closed toilet at the foot of the tub, and gives me his arms to hold on to. His eyes stay trained on my face as we work together to get me standing. I realize halfway up I'm not totally sure I could have done this on my own after all. We might have preemptively saved me from a fall.

He keeps his arm out for me to hold on to while I step out of the tub. For a moment, I'm standing in front of him, water dripping down my naked body. Hunter shakes himself again. That'll bring on a headache if he's not careful.

"Here." He helps me slip on my robe, one arm at a time. I let him move my limbs, happy to cede control for a moment. A gentle push on my shoulder has me spinning to face him. He holds the sides of my robe open for an instant, his gaze traveling one more time from head to toe, before he pulls the robe closed. A gentle yank on the loose ends of the of the sash has me stepping forward into him. My head rests on his chest, my hair soaking his shirt. We stay like that for a moment and I savor the closeness.

His lips press a kiss into my hair before he puts some space between us and ties the sash loosely around my waist. Enough to keep it closed, but not constricting around my growing belly.

"Goodnight, Mich," he says before turning and leaving the bathroom.

"Goodnight, Hunt," I respond, right before the door closes.

It's hard to brush my teeth with a smile trying to force its way onto my face. Smiles are rare these days, but for the first time in weeks, it feels warranted. In those quick moments, I regain a bit of hope. Maybe we can find our back after all.

Twenty~Two

MICHELLE

Twenty-nine weeks pregnant

Hope can suck it.

I throw my phone on the twin bed in Hunter's room.

Hunter
Sorry, a meeting came up I can't miss. Can we do the nursery this weekend?

I ignored my mother's voice in my head calling me a nag when nothing changed after the bathtub moment and started asking if we could work on the nursery. Which involves getting rid of the bed Hunter's been insisting on sleeping in. If that's why he's dragging his feet, or something else, I don't know, because he won't tell me. I'm afraid I'm close to a breaking point where I'll need to decide whether it's healthy to have him living here anymore.

My heart hurts at the thought of him leaving and spurs me into action. No, Hunter, we can't do the nursery this weekend. We're doing it to-fucking-day.

I stand with my hand on my hips, looking at his bed. My gaze lands next on my belly.

Okay, we're doing what I can do on my own right fucking now. If that means it smells like paint fumes while he tries to sleep, so be it. I tuck my phone into my sports bra and survey the room.

Hunter did clear one wall of furniture, so I decide that's the wall I will paint. I manage to lay out a drop cloth and pray I don't drip on the carpet, because there's no fucking way I'm getting down there to tape it to the baseboards.

Part of my mind recognizes I'm making irrational choices right now. I'm going to do a shitty painting job not fully prepping and may create more work in the end. But ask me if I fucking care. I need to do *something*.

I'm bending to pour paint into the tin when the pain hits. A cramp in the lower part of my bump. I straighten, twisting a little bit this way and that, hoping to work it out. The pain flares again.

Okay, no painting. Too much bending. I abandon the open paint can and the tin to be dealt with later and decide to move to the dresser. We've gotten a few things for Cumulus so far. I've washed them, but they've been sitting on top of the dresser since Hunter's clothes are in the drawers. Time to put them away.

The top drawer slides open and I scoop up an armful of boxer briefs, intending to throw them on the bed. They fall to the floor at my feet as the pain appears again, the sharpest yet.

Maybe it's gas. I should try to go to the bathroom. Plus, then, I'm sitting. Win-win.

I walk slowly to the bathroom like any sudden movements may trigger the pain again. I pull down my pants, sit down, and then I see it. A spot of red on my underwear. A smear appears on the toilet paper too.

"Okay, okay. Don't panic." It's time to talk out loud to myself. I pull my phone out and call Hunter. As it rings, I reflect on though things are weird and tense, he's still the one I call first. Voicemail.

I try one more time, hoping to break through Do Not Disturb if it's on. Voicemail after the second ring.

My jaw clenches. I send a text, asking him to call me as soon as he can. I dial a different number.

"Hello?"

"Jax, you answered. Thank fuck."

"Michelle? What's up? Where are you? It sounds all echoey."

"Well, I'm . . . I'm in my bathroom. And . . ." My voice shakes.

"I'm on my way. Keep talking."

"I had a couple pains in my stomach, and now there is some blood. Not a lot, but a little, and everyone knows that's not good . . ."

"Just stole a cab from the Speaker of the House. Senator Marsden's going to hear about that one tomorrow. Why don't you get changed, grab your insurance card, and wait for me on the couch, okay? I'm going to tip the driver fifty if he gets me there in fifteen minutes." A horn blares on Jax's side of the call. "In fifteen minutes *alive*," she emphasizes.

A near traffic accident shouldn't be funny, but I find myself laughing.

"There's my girl," she says. "I'll be there soon, okay?"

Twelve minutes later, Jax is opening my door, using the access code I sent her for the front door. "You don't always leave this unlocked, do you? Of course not. You unlocked it before you sat down. Okay, ready to go? The cab is waiting. I told him we're not playing the speed game on this trip. Don't worry." She wraps her arm around me and locks the door behind me as quickly as she entered.

"Thank you, Jax." It's hard when your social circle has suddenly become people who are connected with your going-through-it boyfriend and you don't know what you should or shouldn't say. Still, the second she knew something was wrong, she dropped who knows what and got here.

"No more thank yous, okay? This is what you do for your people. Let's get you to the hospital. Have you called your OB yet?" A twinge unrelated to whatever's happening with Cumulus goes through my heart. We start down the stairs slowly.

"Michelle, where's Hunter?" The heart twinge intensifies. I think she waited until the stairs to ask so I didn't have to meet her in the eye.

"I don't know. He texted he had some meeting. He might be with Hayden or Duncan or both." I catch her nod once out of the corner of my eye.

"Can I call Charlotte from the cab and do some digging?" We reach the car, which gives me the time until she climbs in the other side to answer.

"Yes, please. Find him. I want . . . I need him here."

That's all she needs before the phone's at her ear. "Charlotte, I need you to find Hayden. Is he with Hunter?" Her answer is muffled. "I'm on the way to the hospital with Michelle. He's not answering our calls." I flash her a grateful smile for leaving out I'm not sure where exactly he is.

I hear Charlotte's voice loud and clear now. "Shit, I'll find them right now. I think I know where the meeting is. I'll head that way now. If Hay doesn't answer, which he fucking better when I call repeatedly, I'll deliver the message in person." The line goes dead.

"You know, I don't think I've ever heard her say fuck before," Jax says, the fondness clear in her voice. This makes me laugh, and she joins me. Her hand reaches across the seat for mine. "Everything's going to be okay."

"You don't know that," I whisper, my hand resting on my stomach. It'll stay there until someone pulls it away.

"You're right," she says, squeezing my hand, right as we pull up to the emergency room. "I really, really hope it will be okay. But if it's not, you're not alone."

CHAPTER
Twenty~Three

HUNTER

Twenty-nine weeks pregnant

The investors are talking with Duncan at the end of the impromptu meeting. I think it went well. All I've been focused on the past few weeks is making this business as successful as I can to support Michelle and our baby. I've taken to picking up kitchen shifts during the day and working through the night. If I can't offer them anything else, at least I can try to provide financial security. But even with that goal at the fore-front, I couldn't tell you what anyone said in this meeting, myself included. My mind's been focused on picturing Michelle's face fall when she got the text canceling our plans to work on the nursery today.

"Shit," Hayden mutters. "I have seven missed calls from Charlotte. And one text saying, 'I'm okay, but I better find you dead or dismembered.'"

"What?" I pull out my phone. Only two calls, but both from Michelle, along with a text that says, "Call me."

Duncan's assistant knocks on the door. "Mr. Brandt?" Three heads swivel in her direction. "There's a Charlotte Reid here to see you?"

"Shit," Hayden mutters, before waving at the room and walking out. Right as the door shuts, I hear Charlotte say. "Go get Hunter."

I'm in the lobby with them before Hayden can open the door again. "What's wrong? It's Michelle. She called, but my phone was on silent."

All the fight drains out of Charlotte, and she leans on Hayden. "Michelle's at the emergency room. GW Hospital. She had some pain and some spotting. They took her back from the waiting room a few minutes ago."

"Fuck." I'm running for the elevator and hear Charlotte and Hayden behind me. "Is she alone?"

Smashing the button over and over isn't making the elevator come any faster. Why the fuck not?

"Jax is with her," Charlotte says as the elevator dings.

"Well thank fuck for that," I mutter, getting in.

"Do you want us to come?" Hayden asks, his eyes full of fear. Gives me a fraction of an idea of what I must look like.

I shake my head. "Later. Go smooth over our exit with the investors, catch Duncan up. Then . . ." The elevator door closes and cuts me off. Hopefully, he caught the gist.

I tumble out onto the street and spot a man getting into a taxi. I rush over. "Sir, can I please have this cab?" He blinks at me blankly. "My girl . . . the love of my life, hospital and our baby. She, she doesn't know I love her." I have no time for cohesive sentences.

He scoffs at me. "This isn't some rom-com. Fuck off." He ducks to get in the cab when a hand reaches for his collar and pulls him out.

"It's not, but it's about to become a *John Wick* movie if you don't give us the fucking cab." Duncan releases the man, who gapes at him like a fish. "That's what I thought." Hayden and

Charlotte come up behind him. "Hunter. Get in the fucking cab. And scoot over."

I do as he says. Charlotte and Hayden climb in after me and Duncan climbs in the front seat.

"Five hundred if you can get us to George Washington Hospital in twenty minutes." A horn honks as the driver swerves into traffic, cutting off a city bus. "Alive," Duncan adds icily, but not clinging to the oh-shit handle like the rest of us.

I try calling Michelle, but it goes straight to voicemail. "Can you get ahold of Jax?" I half yell, not sure who I'm asking.

"I'll keep trying her, but I'm getting voicemail too. Maybe they made them turn their phones off." Charlotte reaches across Hayden to squeeze my hand. "It's going to be okay."

"Are you sure?" I'm okay if she lies to me at this moment.

"I wish I was. But we're here with you, whatever's next."

Hayden puts his hand on top of both of ours. I flashback to when he would crawl into my bed in the weeks after Mom died and cry. I'd hold his hand until he fell asleep, and that's when I would cry. I wonder if he ever knew? We probably haven't had a reason to hold hands since. I meet his eyes, and this time his are dry, while mine aren't. "I don't know what happened on that cruise ship, but you're going to fix it. Today."

He doesn't wait for me to respond, but turns to face the windshield. He's right. I've learned to not trust my gut over the years but decide to throw out the old playbook. I'm going to get the chance to make it right. I know it.

We bust into the emergency department nineteen minutes after leaving Duncan's office building.

I approach the desk, waiting my turn. My weight shifts from foot to foot, trying to breathe deep and remind myself my crisis does not mean any more than the people's in front of me.

"How can I help you?" A dark-skinned woman named Brenda blinks up at me.

"Uh, hi. My name is Hunter Brandt. My . . . my . . ." I stumble over my words as Brenda continues to look less and less impressed with me. "I'm looking for Michelle Lewis. She arrived about an hour ago, with cramping and spotting. Do you know where she is? Can I see her?"

The clack of the keys on Brenda's keyboard is her only response to my question.

"Hmm," she says, and my heart falls into my stomach. Did Michelle tell them to not let me back? I can't believe how royally I fucked this up.

"I see Ms. Lewis put you on the approved persons list. Take this"—she hands me a visitor's badge I hadn't noticed her printing out—"and go through those double doors. She's in bay thirteen."

"Thank you," I say, my heart back firmly in my chest, beating at a rate that seems to indicate I may need a bed myself before this ordeal is over.

She looks down her nose at me from two feet below my eye level. "Get moving, young man."

I spring into action, waving over my shoulder at Hayden, Duncan, and Charlotte. The double doors open slowly. Losing my patience, I squeeze myself through the crack once it's large enough for a human and scan the walls for some sort of way finding.

"Can I help you?" A male nurse in navy scrubs stops next to me.

"Hunter! Down here." I turn to the sound of my name and see Jax waving at me from down the hallway.

"I'm good now, thanks." I turn away from the nurse and make my way to where Jax stands outside what looks like a large, windowed wall, curtains drawn inside the room created by the dividers, so I can't see inside.

"How is she? She's in there? Do they know if she's okay? How's Cumulus?" My words come out in a rush.

"Breathe, Hunt." I take a deep inhale, aware we both hear how shaky it sounded going into my lungs.

"They're examining her now. They had me step outside for the internal exam and ultrasound. I'm really glad you made it."

"Me too. Fuck, we were supposed to work on the nursery today. I should have been here from the beginning."

"Why weren't you? What's going on with you two? Michelle wouldn't give me anything, and I didn't want to press her given"—she waves her hands at our surroundings—"everything. You all have been cryptic ever since the cruise."

It comes pouring out of me. "I fucked everything up. We got kicked off the ship because Michelle was too pregnant to be on a cruise, and I signed the waivers for us without reading them. She got really seasick and dehydrated. She could have died, Jax, and I would have no one to blame but myself because I wanted to be the Prince Charming type and whisk her away on this big adventure. I'm not Prince Charming. I'm the toad, warts and all. I can't take care of a grown woman. What business do I have being a father? So, I've thrown myself into the app and my business. I want to have a chance of giving them something they need. A secure financial future."

Jax crosses her arms and sizes me up. "You know, we don't know each other very well, Hunter, but I'm going to be frank with you. What you just said sounds like some scared chickenshit. Yes, things could have gone medically sideways, but it didn't. Michelle doesn't want your money, she wants you. She needs someone she can count on, to stick with her. So, if you can't do that, if you're going to phone it in with your bank account and nothing else, then you need to turn around and walk yourself out of here." Her eyebrow raises in a move clearly meant to say "your move."

"What if I'm not good enough for her?" I whisper, my

deepest fear tumbling out to my brother's partner, surrounded by the beeps and whirs of hospital equipment.

"Does she make you want to be better?"

I nod. "Every fucking day."

"Then go in there. And be better. One thing I've learned about life is most people have no idea what they're doing. But as long they're not doing it alone, they can make it through."

I pull Jax into a bone-crushing hug, hearing her "oof" seconds before she wraps her arms around me to squeeze me back, patting me between the shoulder blades a few times before breaking my hold.

"Thanks, Jax."

"Don't mention it. I owed Michelle breakdown support. You guys are a package deal now."

Part of the wall next to us opens, revealing a door into the exam room. A young doctor with tan skin, teal scrubs, and his hair covered in a tie-dye cap walks out and stops short when he sees us.

"Oh, hi. Dad?" His eyes meet mine. I nod. "I'm Dr. Munoz. I'm waiting for a second opinion on the sonogram, but I'll be right back to talk to you both momentarily. You can head on in."

I look at Jax, unsure if she wants to go in first. "Go," she shoos me, turning to walk out toward the waiting room.

One more deep inhale and I knock on the door, pushing it open slowly.

"I'm not really sure why he made you leave. You could have stayed up by my head . . ." Michelle's voice trails off as her head turns and spots me in the doorway instead of Jax. "Oh, hi." Her uncertainty is written all over her face.

I take in the scene in front of me. The charts and numbers flashing on the screen from the monitors hooked up to Michelle. The way the blanket covers her now popped baby bump, the contrast against the bright white sheets of her red hair. Her skin is paler than usual, but her blue eyes are clear.

"Baby," I say, crossing the room in an instant, grabbing the hand without an IV in it. I place a kiss on the back of it before gripping our clasped hands to my chest. "I'm so fucking sorry."

Her eyes fill, a few tears spilling over. "I'm so glad you're here," she whispers.

My body bends forward over the railing of the bed so my forehead meets hers. "I shouldn't have been anywhere else. You and Cumulus . . . you're the most important things in the world to me. I know I've been shit at showing it lately, but no more."

"You've been so distant. I thought I did something wrong, or you didn't want me, want us, anymore." The pain in her voice threatens to break me in two.

I draw away enough to be sure she can see my eyes, read my sincerity in them. "You didn't do anything wrong. That was about me. After the cruise, when I put you in danger . . . it shook me. What if I couldn't hack it? What if you and Cumulus were better off with me? So, I threw myself into the business. If you can't count on me to do the right thing, I could at least provide you with security." A line of moisture trails down my cheek. She reaches up to wipe it away, her hand lingering on my face.

"Hunt, my job is literally trying to use science to predict the future. If I needed certainty in my life, I would have been an accountant."

A laugh bursts from me, surprising both of us. I spent the last thirty minutes in hell unsure if I would ever laugh again. "I will spend every day for the rest of my life making sure you know I'm here for you, I'm in this." She inhales sharply, surprise on her face at my declaration. I decide to go for broke. "Michelle, I—"

"Knock, knock,"

Dr. Munoz enters the room, breaking the moment. We both turn to look his way.

"Sorry for the wait, folks. Like I said after the sonogram, her heart rate is strong, and she's doing okay. I wanted to speak to one of my colleagues about recommendations for next steps."

"She?" I ask, plopping into the chair conveniently placed behind me. Probably for moments like this one.

Anxiety crosses Michelle's face. "Sorry, I know we were waiting to find out, but when everything was happening, and I wasn't sure what was next, I wanted to know more about Cumulus, about her. So, I asked."

"That's amazing. It's a girl. I'm so fucked," I say, a laugh-sob breaking free from my chest as tears flow freely now. Michelle squeezes my hand.

Dr. Munoz laughs softly. "I'm a girl dad too. But my wife and my husband get to be the fun ones, while I have to lay down the law or else they'd never eat anything green, and we'd need a bigger house."

We both laugh along with him.

"What happens next?" Michelle asks.

"We recommend you get in touch with your OB and set up weekly visits from now until you deliver. Take it easy for a few days. We can write you a note for work if you need it. And"—his eyes dart between us—"I would recommend pelvic rest until you're back with your doctor and able to get their final recommendation."

Michelle and Dr. Munoz talk about getting the information to her doctor while I pull out my phone and run a quick search. Pelvic rest means what I thought it did—no penetrative sex. Michelle's and Cumulus's health is way more important than getting my dick wet. I'll swear off orgasms for the rest of the year. Hell longer, if it means baby girl comes without any further complications. But I've only had one chance to worship her body since our first night together. If she lets me touch her again, I want to be sure we're being safe.

"We're going to get the discharge paperwork finished up, and you'll be on your way shortly. Let me know if you have any questions before you go."

We both nod and thank him for his time. Then, it's the two of us again.

"A girl," I whisper, and Michelle nods, a huge smile taking over her face. "We better get down to work narrowing those names. And should we return the paint? Change the nursery theme?"

"No," she shakes her head. "I think we should stick with our theme. I'm absolutely going to buy cute headbands for her to wear but also don't want to put too many gender norms on her from birth. She can be who she'll be."

I nod, wondering once again why someone as fan-fucking-tastic as this woman lets me be a part of this.

"Do you mind going to get me a glass of water? They were running liquid through here"—she holds up her hand with an IV in it—"but my throat is so dry. I'd love something to drink."

"Of course." I jump up, before bending down to brush a kiss to her forehead. "I'll be back before you know it."

Out in the hall, I ask a passing nurse where I can find a glass of water. She tells me she'll be back with a cup of ice and a cup of water. While I'm waiting, Dr. Munoz comes around the corner.

"Hey, uh, Doc?" I say, flagging him down. "Quick question. About the pelvic rest—if she needs for the rest of the pregnancy, does that mean no . . ." I clear my throat and look around. "Sexual stimulation at all for the rest of pregnancy?"

The doctor shows off his bright white teeth with a broad smile. "Hold off on anything until you get to her OB, but it's likely a restriction on penetration only. Other types of stimula-tion, and orgasms, should be just fine. Encouraged even." The doctor winks at me, and I catch the purple, blue, and pink lanyard peeking out of his pocket.

"Right on," I say, and the doctor claps me on the shoulder before walking away as the nurse returns with our water.

I return to the room where Michelle gladly takes a sip of water before starting to chew on some ice chips. My phone vibrates for the umpteenth time since I've been back here, and I pull it out.

"Are you okay if I update everyone to let them know they can go home and we'll talk to them tomorrow?"

"Everyone?" she asks, looking up from her cup of ice.

"Yeah, Duncan and Hayden were with me when Charlotte found us. I'm guessing Jax is still with them too."

"They all came?" Her eyes are open with wonder.

"I'm not sure I wouldn't have vibrated apart without Hayden holding my hand on the way over here," I say, unashamed to admit the depth of my fear. "But they were so worried too. Of course they're here."

"Oh," Michelle says. "Maybe they can come over for brunch on Sunday?"

I smile and start a new group chat, combining all four of my brothers, plus Charlotte, Jax, and Michelle. Her phone buzzes in her lap, laughing as she unlocks it, and it continues to vibrate with messages coming in fast and furious.

"Welcome to the Brandt brothers group chat, Michelle. It's possible you're going to want to mute the thread, but they say brunch on Sunday sounds great, as long as you're feeling okay."

Michelle laughs again as she reads all the messages, presumably of everyone sharing their relief at the good news and catching Spencer up on what he's missed over the past few hours.

A nurse comes through the door and hands me a packet of papers. She moves to remove the IV and tapes gauze over the back of Michelle's hand. "You're all set to get dressed and head out whenever you're ready. Good luck!"

She leaves again, no doubt to tend to someone who needs her attention more than we do. I know I have work to do to win back Michelle's trust, but for the first time in weeks, I have hope.

Michelle pulls her leggings on and picks up her bag. I walk over and grab the tote from her, swinging it over my shoulder and pulling her into my side. She sighs, a weary sound, and leans into me.

"Hunter?"

"Yeah?" I say, pressing a kiss to the crown of her head, because I can.

"Let's go home."

We walk out, side by side, and I'm positive every patient we pass knows we got good news from the size of the smile on my face. Yeah, I think we might be all right.

CHAPTER

Twenty~Four

MICHELLE

Thirty-two weeks pregnant

It's been three weeks since my ER trip. Things with Cumulus have felt normal since. Well as much as carrying around a papaya on the front of your body can be normal. I caught Dr. Barber on my first visit after the ER and she spent almost thirty minutes with me, going over the doctor's notes and taking a look at everything herself. She wants me to continue with the weekly visits and has recommended taking it easy where I can. But she did remove me from pelvic rest.

I haven't told Hunter yet. He's been at every doctor's appointment since, but the first one came via a same day opening I took advantage of when I heard the slot belonged to Dr. Barber. Hunter was on the line with Duncan, canceling his morning meeting when I told him to go ahead and go. He had barely left my side since the ER, and I needed a bit of space for when I talked to the doctor again. I told him everything else. Showed him the new sonogram pictures and breathed in his cedar scent when he hugged me after I reported the good news. Well, ninety percent of the good news.

I know in my rational brain, Hunter is all in. My heart warms when I remember him painting the nursery, making me watch from the hallway under a blanket and through a mask while he shivered through the cold October day with the window wide open. His meals are becoming comfort food based, while also somehow remaining healthy and full of good things pregnant moms need. The light I put in his eyes when I told him he should partner with an OB to make a pregnancy line of meal plans fought away the cold and rainy grey days we've had for the last week.

But I'm still holding back. I keep hearing him say "for the rest of my life" and wondering if the "I" statement interrupted in the ER was "I love you." Did his emotions from the day get the best of him? Does he really mean it? I want to believe him so badly, but a voice that sounds a lot like my mother's tells me he'll withdraw again as soon as I do.

"So, I had another session with my new therapist today." Hunter kicks off the dinner conversation. Yes, he found a therapist to work through the feelings of unworthiness and fear of failure that caused him to pull away. Seriously, what is wrong with me again?

"Do you still think it's a good fit?" I ask, moaning around a mouth full of mashed potatoes. Hunter pauses for a second, his eyes drawn to my lips around the spoon. I know I should tell him. But our bodies communicating has never been the problem. It's our hearts, our brains, and our words that need to get on the same page.

"Yeah, I really am. Weekly sessions seemed like a lot at first, but I'm glad it's how we're starting. There's a lot of background to get through. Duncan had her number a little too ready, given she specializes in unprocessed adolescent grief. It's like he's been waiting for this or something."

"Or he's seen her himself," I say mindlessly, watching

Hunter's eyes widen as he processes. "You can't ask him." I say immediately, and Hunter nods, his face full of understanding. "But maybe you can mention to him in a few weeks how much it's helping and see if he wants to share in return."

"Gosh, you're smart," he says, offering me more potatoes and scooping them onto my plate when I nod.

"Decades of therapy myself at work." Hunter's eyes fill with understanding. We've had some good talks about our childhoods in the past few weeks at the suggestion of Hunter's therapist. He explained how, growing up, he felt left out, which led to acting out and then branding himself a screw up and a failure. I shared more about my mom's dating history and how that imprinted some abandonment issues on me his behavior triggered. See, hearts and brains, communicating.

"So, what's the plan for trick-or-treating tomorrow?" Jax, Preston, and Laurel's boss, the senator from Rhode Island, tasked his staff with running trick-or-treating at his row house on Capitol Hill tomorrow night. Something about not being able to be in two places at once and not needing the negative press the week before the election claiming he doesn't care about children.

Hunter lets me change the subject. "We're supposed to be there at five. Our costumes got couriered over this afternoon." A bag I didn't notice when I got home lands on the empty chair between us. "I still say *Wizard of Oz* is out and *Wicked* is in, but it sounds like your cousin is a traditionalist." He hands a folded brown fuzzy pile to me.

"She watched *The Wizard of Oz* every day when we were kids. Took her six months to not hide her face every time the Wicked Witch came on the screen." I hold up my Cowardly Lion onesie, happy to have something comfortable and simple for Halloween this year.

"And now she's dying to be green, apparently." He holds up the plaid shirt, straw hat, and suspenders. His own jeans will suffice for his scarecrow costume. "She's not serious with this, right?" His hand removes a bundle of hay from the bottom of the bag.

"Deadly, I'm afraid." I giggle. "And besides, her being the Wicked Witch is where the *Wicked* tie-in comes in. You know everyone shipped Glinda and Elphaba after the movie came out. Making Caitlin play Glinda to her Elphaba feels like some sort of drawn out, public foreplay."

He shrugs. "I respect the commitment to the bit."

"Be sure you have that hay sticking out of places you'll be able to stand it all night. I promise she'll have backup hay to stuff down your pants if you don't."

Hunter shudders. "Duly noted."

As twilight falls over the city blocks shadowed by the Capitol, children and parents are out in droves. They dart over sidewalks, shrieking in joy at whatever treat they discover in the next courtyard they enter.

I have to hand it to Laurel; everyone looks fantastic. Her green skin paint may forever dye their shower, but it will have been worth it as she stands in a black dress and hat next to her wife, Caitlin, who's gamely wearing a bright pink dress with her black braided hair gathered in a high pony-tail. Jax's pigtails and blue checked jumper have Preston looking like he wants to use tin man outfit to power him and Jax right out of there and into bed. When Laurel gives him a hard time about not using the silver face paint she provided, he sagely points out at least one of them shouldn't have an altered skin color heading into election week.

I sit in a chair and take in the scene. Hunter stands next to the large cauldron full of candy, passing treats out to those who can't quite reach the lip. He is fully committed, keeping his arms stick straight and bending at the waist when dropping candy into waiting buckets, much to the giggles and delight of the tiny recipients. A different kind of warmth spreads through my body watching him. Once I'm positive I haven't accidentally wet myself, I have to acknowledge the feeling for what it is—something a lot like love. Eight months ago, I'd never have dared to dream the handsome, yet closed-off, tattooed man who rocked my world would be gamely participating in a group costume and giving it his all.

Hunter catches me watching him, and flashes a brilliant smile my way, only causing the warmth in my chest to expand. He calls to Preston to take over cauldron duty and plops down in the chair next to me.

"Good call separating Dorothy and the Tin Man there. I worried things were about to get a little bit too adult."

"Yeah, must be election week stress. Knowing my brother has a thing for handlebars is knowledge I could have lived the rest of my life without."

I smack him gently. "Calling pigtails handlebars? What are you, sixteen?"

He laughs and captures my hand, keeping it in his lap. His thumb rubs gently across my skin.

"So, next Halloween. You, me, and princess Cumulus. What do you think our group costume should be? Because I've made a note of at least five or six ideas from what I've seen around tonight. Only we'd be way better at them."

I stare over at him, watching the open joy on his face as he follows the groups of families and friends on the sidewalk. He must realize I never answered, because he looks at me in question.

"What? Oh. Did you already have an idea in mind? We can do yours, for sure. We have a lot of Halloweens to look forward to." He presses a kiss on the back of my hand and returns it to his lap, enclosing it on both sides as he brings his other hand to join our embrace.

He talks about our future like it's a foregone conclusion. It rekindles my kernel of hope into a full-blown flame.

"Mich?" His face looks quizzical. I realize I've been quiet for too long.

"I think I love you," I blurt out, my cheeks immediately flaming.

"You think so, do you?" he asks with the smirk that could melt a million panties firmly in place. But I want it directed only at me from now on.

"Well, that's convenient. Because I know I love you." He leans forward and taking my mouth in a soft, but all-consuming kiss. He puts his love into each pass of his lips.

Someone outside the fence cat calls, and we pull away slowly, our foreheads tipping together, smiles blindingly large.

"Yeah, I'd read that fanfic," Laurel says from behind Hunter, and our whole group laughs as I settle under his arm against his side. My hand settles on my stomach, Cumulus moving around more than usual. It's a milder Halloween evening, but the warmth of hearing this man, the father of my baby girl, a cornerstone of our family, cares about me could keep me warm in the coldest of nights.

Epistolary Interlude #3

BRANDT BROTHERS AND PARTNERS GROUP CHAT

Duncan
Everyone knows their assignments for dinner tomorrow?

Spencer
How did Duncan get put in charge of a Thanksgiving dinner not being held in one of his apartments? I'm pretty sure he hasn't cooked himself a meal in a decade.

Jax
I wasn't stopping him.

Preston
I wasn't stopping him.

Charlotte
Cuties.

Michelle and Jax, have they warned you about twenty questions and being ready to say what you're thankful for?

Jax
What's that now?

Michelle
Tell me more.

Spencer
You're letting them in on trade secrets.

Hayden
Don't worry, we won't warn anyone you ever bring to Thanksgiving dinner.

Spencer
Yeah, that'll happen anytime soon. Everyone in my lab is married to science, someone else, or aromantic. And considering I only leave the lab to see you people . . .

Preston
Awe, buddy. Want to talk about it?

Spencer
Definitely not.

Michelle
So, this twenty question thing. Should I be worried?

Hunter
Definitely.

But don't worry, I'll protect you.

Charlotte
I held my own pretty well. I'm sure they can
handle it.

Hayden
Anyone want to put wagers on the football
games tomorrow?

Duncan
This is great and all, but no one has answered
my question about the food.

Preston
Guys, he's going to fire another assistant if we
don't respond.

Charlotte
Got it!

Hunter

Spencer

Jax

Duncan
Finally. Now, was that so hard?

CHAPTER

Twenty~Five

HUNTER

Thirty-six weeks pregnant

"You know, I don't mean to sound ungrateful Duncan rented this beautiful space for our baby shower today. But asking a woman this pregnant to drive more than five miles in city traffic should be examined by the Geneva code."

I meet the alarmed eyes of our ride share driver in the rearview mirror. I shoot him what I hope is a reassuring smile, hoping he bites his tongue about how we've only actually traveled a little over two miles. Traffic is awful. Taking the Metro may have been faster, but is not Michelle's current favorite mode of transportation.

"Just another block or so babe, and then we'll find a bathroom."

She looks over at me, horrified. "Please never tell Duncan I said that. I'm really excited about today. It's uncomfortable having a head of romaine lettuce sitting on my bladder."

"It'll be our secret. Let this experience solidify if you ever mention anything you'd like to do or anywhere you'd like to go in

199

front of Duncan, he'll do everything in his power to make it happen." Duncan rented out the tearoom at The Willard for our baby shower after Michelle mentioned in passing she always wanted to do an afternoon tea. I squeeze her hand.

"Well, next time, I'll shoot a little higher and say Paris or something." She squeezes my hand and dazzles me with her smile. Michelle's pretty uncomfortable all the time now, but I can't help staring at her whenever I have the chance. She's glowing and gorgeous, more and more every day.

"Here we are," our driver says. I jump out and run around the car to open Michelle's door and help her maneuver her way to standing.

"Thanks, man," I say, and give a higher than usual tip for the trouble of worrying an accident would occur in his back seat any moment.

We walk into the lobby of The Willard and Michelle stops dead, taking in the ornate carvings on the ceiling and marble columns. I spot a discreetly placed sign directing us to the restroom.

"We better head this way, babe." I put pressure on her back and point us in the direction of the ladies' room.

"Yes, right. Wow, it's so beautiful in here. It made me forget how badly I have to pee. Would be a shame to get kicked out for soiling the floor before I can enjoy the spread, wouldn't it?" She picks up the pace and disappears behind a thick oak door.

I wait for her, checking on a few emails and tagging a few things for my assistant to deal with at the end of the weekend. After the scare at the emergency room, Duncan insisted on giving me more funds so I could hire an assistant, as well as made me promise I'd quit picking up jobs in kitchens. I insisted he take an additional five percent of the company but am doing a much better job of balancing all of my priorities, with Michelle at the forefront.

My phone buzzes with a text from Charlotte, letting me

know the room is ready for us whenever we arrive. Michelle appears at my side a moment later.

"All right, let's get this over with," she says, something between a smile and a grimace on her face. I hold out my elbow and she tucks her hand in as we start walking to the elevator.

"Remember, say the word, and we're out of here," I say, pushing the button for the Mezzanine level where the tearoom is located.

"No, I'm really touched the girls and Margaret want to do this for me, especially on Thanksgiving weekend. You'd think with being on TV for as long as I have, I wouldn't mind the spotlight, but there I have more of a purpose than as an incubator." She rests her free hand on her stomach.

"Hey." I pull gently on her arm, bringing us to a stop and turning to face her. "You know I hate hearing you talk like that. You are so much more than these forty weeks of your life. What's really going on?"

She huffs out a breath. "I think I'm struggling knowing my mom won't be here. I put off telling her about you and Cumulus for so long because I didn't need her negativity, but then too much time passed. Though, I'm not sure why I'm worried about her feelings when she didn't bother calling on Thanksgiving. A tornado of emotions in here." She taps at her head.

I pull her into me, pressing a kiss to the top of her head. "Well, pull me into your funnel cloud. I never want you to face gale force winds alone." We stand there for a minute before her shoulders start shaking and I hear her giggling.

"What?" I ask, pulling back to look at her face. Her laughter is contagious.

"You are being really cute and sweet. I'm being mean."

I raise an eyebrow. "What, because gale force winds aren't as strong as the wind speeds with a tornado?"

She nods, her eyes shining. "Did you do that on purpose?"

I shrug. "A gentleman doesn't weather talk and tell. Ready to greet your adoring public?"

Michelle nods and reaches up on her tiptoes to place a peck on my mouth. "With you, I'm ready for anything."

We reach the tearoom, which Duncan alluded he traded many favors to book for us this weekend, and find it already full of people mulling around.

"She's here!" Laurel shrieks, moving toward us at a pace I'm sure is outside decorum for this space on a normal day. Everyone's attention is pulled toward the door, and people filter to greet us.

Dad, Margaret, and my siblings are all here, plus Charlotte and Jax. Caitlin waves from where she's rearranging the presents on a table from across the room. Some of Michelle's colleagues have settled at one of the tables decorated in a sage green, with dusty rose accents, digging into a tower of finger sandwiches. A few other people I don't recognize are milling around, but my eyes snag on the woman with bright red hair standing talking to our neighbor from across the hall. The color is striking and so familiar.

"Fuck." Michelle breathes as she stands next to me looking in the same direction. "Ready for anything but that."

"Is that . . ." I ask as the woman in question turns around and I see Michelle's nose and eyes present on a woman in her late fifties.

"Yup, that's my mom," Michelle says through her teeth. A glance her way shows a forced smile as she waves in her mom's direction. The two women start making their way to us and sweat starts to form in my armpits. Fuck, how do I not know Michelle's mom's name? Is her last name Lewis? I think Michelle said she'd been married at least once? Or maybe just an engagement?

Michelle squeezes my arm before stepping forward. Fuck, I should be supporting her right now, not the other way around. I step next to her, my hand on her back to assure her we've got this together.

"Mom, hi!" Michelle says, holding her arms out for a hug her mother limply returns. Her mom's eyes flash to mine, and in that instant, I know she's pissed.

"I found your mom knocking on your door a little while ago," Nancy, the woman from 2B, says to us. "I told her I was on my way here, if she wanted to take the Metro with me since she'd gotten the time wrong."

"Well, thanks so much for rescuing her, Nancy," Michelle says, her voice one I recognize from when she's calling for sunny skies, knowing there's the smallest chance an isolated thunderstorm could break out and turn the whole day to hell. "Mom, I'd like you to meet Hunter. Hunter, this is my mom, Diana Lewis."

Diana. Same last name. I commit it to memory now. "It's so nice to meet you, Ms. Lewis," I say, reaching out for a hug, only to be rebuffed with a handshake. All right then.

"I moved recently and am having trouble with my mail forwarding. Michelle told me the time, but I must have written it down wrong. I'm so grateful you were there, so I didn't miss this special occasion in my daughter's life." Diana's voice is laced with something so poisonous it almost sounds sweet.

Nancy must only pick up on the honey as she beams at us, still under the impression she's provided a great service. "Well, I'm off to grab a clothespin. Make sure you get one Diana—but don't say baby!"

"I think I'll find I'm biting my tongue all over the place today," Diana says, her eyes skating over me. Her expression displays she's not impressed with what she sees.

"So, you moved?" Michelle says as Nancy walks away, her tone conversational, with a side of optimism.

"Of course not. I assumed you didn't want your guests to know you're the type of person who doesn't invite your own mother to your baby shower. A shower for a baby you didn't bother to tell me existed."

Michelle looks like she took a punch to the stomach, her face falling. I watch as she curls in on herself, unsure what role I should play in stopping it. "Sorry, Mom. I meant to tell you, but

I know you have your own brand of advice about relationships. I thought it might be easier if Hunter and I navigated things on our own for a while."

"Ah, yes. Hunter. You're certainly a colorful one, aren't you?" Her eyes fall to where my sleeves are visible under my rolled-up cuffs. "But I can see what you see in him, Michelle." Diana gestures all around. "Seems like he comes with a lot of perks and benefits."

"Oh, well Hunter's brother reserved this—" I wince as a mean smile crosses Diana's face.

"Oh, Hunter's brother reserved the space. So his family could be involved as you navigated *things*"—her eyes flick to Michelle's stomach with disdain—"between the two of you. With a brother like that I understand why you wanted to get knocked up. But you know very well a baby doesn't guarantee a man will stay. We're living proof."

I've had enough. I step closer to tuck Michelle under my shoulder. "Hey—"

Clinking of metal on china rings through the room, cutting me off. Charlotte stands at the front, teacup and fork in hand, waiting for everyone to turn her way.

"Thank you everyone for coming out today to shower Michelle and Hunter ahead of the arrival of their little one. The tea is fully steeped and the sandwiches are waiting, so grab a seat and let's dig in. Guests of honor, you're up here!" Charlotte indicates to a sweetheart table up near the present table.

"Look, Mom. I don't want to do this with you right now. You're welcome to stay, but please, if you're going to be mad, be mad at me. Don't take it out on anyone else."

Diana ponders for a second, then her face transforms into something pleasant and friendly. "Guess I better go get a clothespin then. The bar downstairs doesn't open for another couple of hours, anyway. Might as well drink some fancy ass tea." She walks away, taking a seat next to Nancy. Whatever she says,

Nancy must respond with the word "baby" as Diana wags her finger and takes the clothespin from the other woman's collar.

"Are you sure you're okay with her staying?" I say, as we move slowly to our table. "This place must have staff who knows how to get someone out without making a scene."

Michelle shakes her head, taking a few deep breaths. "No. I said earlier I felt weird she wasn't here, right? I spoke it into existence, and now I have to deal with it. Let's go eat some tiny sandwiches, cookies, and open some hopefully adorable ass clothes."

She smiles up at me, and only months of reading every emotion in her face betrays how close she is to falling apart. But I decide not to argue, instead helping Michelle scoot her chair in closer to the table. The whole time my eyes are on Diana, determined to watch her like a hawk.

CHAPTER
Twenty-Six

MICHELLE

Thirty-six weeks pregnant

While I don't love sitting in front of everyone so they can watch me eat, I do appreciate Hunter isn't forcing me to make small talk. I can't believe my mom showed up uninvited. I realize we didn't talk about why she's in town, but it's not totally out of character for her to show up unannounced. It's never come with such a large stake attached before.

"Hey, Mich," Hunter says my name in a way that tells me it's not the first time he's said it. "Try to eat something, okay?" He looks worried.

I nod, grabbing a cucumber sandwich from our tower. "Thanks, babe." I reach over and squeeze his knee. He wraps his pinky around mine and our hands dangle between us. Hunter keeps eating with his left hand, wanting to be sure I know he's right here.

"Michelle." I jump slightly as Jax lays her hand on my shoulder. "Shit, sorry. Didn't mean to scare you. We're going to do presents soon. Charlotte suggested I see if you need to go to the bathroom beforehand."

"Well, I didn't before, but I do now." I laugh. "Is there anything she doesn't think of?"

"If so, I haven't found it yet," Jax says. "Hunter, Margaret wants to ask you something, too." She nods to where his stepmom sits with his dad, Spencer, and Duncan.

"Okay," he says. He turns to me and says, "See you in a minute?" before placing a kiss right at the corner of my mouth.

I nod and get up, making my way slowly to the bathroom, my hand on my lower back as I walk across the hall.

Pinching my cheeks to bring a bit of color to them after I wash my hands, I meet my eyes in the mirror and steel myself. *A little bit longer, and then you can go home, put on sweatpants, and ask Hunter to rub your feet.* I give myself a nod and am checking my purse for my Chapstick when I run into the door, hitting someone standing too close to the entrance.

"Oh, shit, sorry . . ." I trail off, swallowing and pulling my chin up when I see who's waiting for me. I should have seen this coming. "Okay, Mom. Let's have it. Why are you here?"

She rolls her eyes, like I'm the one who confronted her in a hallway. "No need to be so dramatic. Am I not allowed to come to town to see my daughter?"

"Of course you are. I thought we were passed the whole showing up unannounced thing, though. You said you had plans for Thanksgiving, so I didn't expect you to make a trip anytime soon."

Her hand waves in the air like she's trying to brush away cigarette smoke. "Oh, Ed's long gone. The girls and I spent the day at the casino. I suppose you and your little boy toy were with his family in there?"

Ah. That helps explain why her words have extra venom today. She and her latest fling split up. It's probably uncharitable to think about your mother, but I'm guessing he left her.

"Yes, Preston and his partner hosted in their building's club house. It seems to be a new family tradition. I made your apple pie." I offer up an olive branch.

She snorts. "What, an apple pie from the supermarket?"

I nod. "Don't tell Hunter. He's a chef and might die a little. I told him I baked it while he was out, though he might not believe me. I did take it out of the Wegmans container and put it in a baking dish." I watch as my mother's face shutters. Shit, why did I say the store?

"Wegmans, huh? Guess that rich boy and you share that healthy food habit you always went on about growing up? Is that where you met him, in the aisles? Your organic baguettes cross?"

Once I finish processing this new entry into the mom trauma diaries, I need to make a note to tell Jax that one as a meet cute for one of her stories. "No, we didn't meet at the supermarket." I dread telling her where we did meet.

"So, where then? Bar? A club? Online? Hot Yoga?" She keeps going as I catch Jax standing behind her. Her face is full of questions about whether she should interrupt. I shake my head no and she looks pained, but walks away.

My shake isn't as subtle as I thought.

"Okay, fine, it doesn't matter where you met him. What's your plan when he leaves? You can come home, live with me, and run your little weather internet videos from Kansas." She seems sincere in this offer, but I can't believe she's this delusional.

"What? I haven't lived in the Midwest in almost twenty years, Mom. And besides"—I shake my head, angry that's the part I addressed first—"he's not going to leave. What Hunter and I have is strong. It's real. I know you don't like to trust things can last, but this is different. We can."

She rolls her eyes again. "That's what they all say."

My mind catches up to the other thing she said when suggesting I move home. "Wait, you've seen my weather videos? You said you hate how scientific I make everything." Probably another reason it hurt so much when the station made me adjust my on-air forecasts.

"Oh, I still think it sounds like you're making up words. But my friends kept sending me those links, so I finally watched some, and then went back and watched some more. And you know what I noticed? Your curves changing. I'm your mother. Of course I knew."

I reel back like she slapped me. "So, you came here knowing I'm pregnant? You planned to ambush me and give me a hard time about this?"

She shrugs. "Maybe. Crashing your baby shower made getting the lay of the land easier. I can tell, Michelle, these are not our people. His family will abandon you when he does."

"No, they won't." Hunter appears suddenly at my side. Where the fuck did he come from? "Even if something happens between Michelle and me, which I don't plan to ever let happen, my family would still love and care for Michelle and our daughter, because that's what loving someone is. It's not something you have to seek out or chase but given freely."

I'm not sure I've ever seen my mother look more offended. "I'm her mother. You think I don't love her? I'm the only family she has."

"I'm not saying you don't, but what I'm watching right now? This isn't love. And you're not the only family she has anymore." Hunter nods to the small crowd gathered at the other end of the hallway—his siblings and partners, Laurel and Caitlin. "She's one of us now. If she decides to let you, we'll welcome you in and love you, too. But it's going to be up to her."

He wraps his arm around me and pulls me close. "Now, for the well-being of the woman I love and our daughter, I need you to leave."

The same blue eyes I see in the mirror every day meet mine, a question in them. Am I going to let this man send her away? I keep eye contact, but don't say anything.

"Fine," she huffs. "The food here tastes disgusting anyway. I guess I'll wait for a birth announcement."

"We'll be in touch," Hunter says, and I squeeze his waist.

My mom walks away in a huff. Laurel steps forward with her coat and purse. "Here you go, *Aunt* Diana." My mother wrenches them away from her and walks around the corner without a second look.

"No other family? I'm literally her cousin, standing right here," Laurel says, failing to keep her voice down.

"So not the time, babe," Caitlin says, but it breaks the mood, and I start laughing. After a moment though, the laughter stops and the tears come. Hunter cups my face and pulls me into him.

"I think we need to take a rain check on those presents," I hear him say over my head.

"Of course," Charlotte responds. "You guys get home. We'll figure everything else out."

"I'll go run and get your stuff," Laurel says, and I hear her shoes clacking at a pace that tells me she's actually running.

I wipe under my eyes and turn to face my friends. "I'm really sorry you all had to hear that."

"I'm sorry you had to live with that," Spencer says, and Duncan elbows him. "What? We were all thinking it."

A wet laugh-sob combo leaves me. Laurel returns with our jackets and my bag and throws her arms around me, pushing Hunter off. "Love you, cuz. Lunch soon?"

"Love you, too. You've got it."

Waving to everyone else, I let Hunter guide me to the elevator and follow him to the sidewalk and into a taxi on autopilot. He somehow manages to buckle himself into the middle seat so I can lay my head on his shoulder and close my eyes. "Let's go home."

Thirty minutes later, I've scrubbed my face clean of makeup, twisted my hair into a bun, and have on the comfy two-piece maternity lounge set from Costco I bought in all three colors. This one's a jewel green.

"I love you in this color," Hunter says from the couch. He's changed into grey sweatpants and a tight white T-shirt, showing off more of the ink on his arms, and a hint of the color on his shoulders through the thin fabric. He pats the couch next to him, and I waddle over and sink down.

"Do you want to talk about it?"

"Not even a little bit," I say, scrunching up my face.

"Got it. I felt like I needed to ask."

"And I love you for it." I lean over to peck him on the lips, lingering for two or three more kisses before he pulls away.

"So, what do you want to do? Order in takeout? Foot rub? Movie marathon of your choosing? An orgasm or two? Anything and everything is on the table."

I laugh and lay my head on his shoulder, hating I had to move it to get out of the car and change. "Definitely takeout, because you never offer that. Then, movie and foot rub for sure. Let's see how the food settles and what pressure points you hit. The orgasm might be necessary."

"Here." He hands me his phone. "We'll divide and conquer. Pick out what you want to eat. I'll start rubbing and then the orgasms can start before the food gets here."

"This is why you're going to conquer the meal planning world. You're a genius." We rearrange so my feet are in his lap, and my back is up against the side of the couch. His thumbs get to work, and from the first second his hands are on me, I'm positive even without the baby hormones, this would end in orgasms. My eyes close and my head tilts back, forgetting I'm supposed to be looking for food.

A knock at the door startles us both.

"Did you order food by osmosis?"

I look down at the phone, making sure I didn't pregnancy

brain my way into ordering something and losing track of time. "Nope, that's not from me."

"Maybe they'll go away," he says, resuming his rubbing.

"We know you're in there. Open up."

"Spencer?" Hunter says, putting my feet on the couch and getting up to open the door.

"Listen," Spencer says as he tumbles in the door, followed by a parade of Brandts, plus Charlotte, Jax, Laurel, and Caitlin. "If you hate this idea, they talked me into it. But if you love it, I want all the credit."

Jax rolls her eyes, adopting the exasperated older sister look very well for an only child. I'll have to get her to teach me. "What Spencer is trying to say is we hated you didn't get to finish your party. We needed to bring the presents over at some point anyway, so we thought we'd see if you wanted to open them now, in front of a smaller crowd. Nancy let us in. She feels awful about bringing your mom to the shower."

"Besides, we have this cake Duncan paid the hotel an arm and leg for." Preston sets it down on the coffee table.

Duncan takes his jacket off and sets it on the back of one of my dining chairs before sitting in it. It's probably the most causal I've ever seen him, including Thanksgiving dinner on Thursday. "It was only an arm. You need to watch such overexaggeration in the House, Prez."

Hunter looks at me and I shrug. He smiles and moves to the kitchen to start getting plates and silverware for the cake. Margaret takes over getting chairs in from the table, and Caitlin organizes the presents again, this time on the floor in front of me. Jax and Charlotte sit on the floor on the other side of the table, continuing a discussion started on the way over. Stephen and Hayden laugh over something Preston said. My heart grows three sizes like the Grinch's. Though in my case, I think I had a lot of heart to begin with. But now, it pushes against the edges of my ribcage, threatening to overflow and fill the rest of my body.

Hunter sits down next to me and watches me taking in everyone around us. "Like I said, you're one of us now."

I bury my face in his shoulder, overcome for a moment, before I take a deep breath and reengage with the rest of the room.

"Someone said something about cake?"

Laurel squeezes in on my other side and hands me the piece Jax cut for me. The cake may be the best thing I've ever tasted, surrounded by the large family I've always wanted.

CHAPTER
Twenty-Seven

HUNTER

Thirty-eight weeks pregnant

"Hunter, I think my water broke."

Of course, tonight has to be the first December snowstorm DC has seen in over a decade. I peek out the window at the white covered streets from our bedroom while Michelle changes her pants. Best I can tell, they haven't seen a plow in a few hours.

"How are we ever going to get a car to come pick us up in this?" She paces around the room grabbing things I'm positive are duplicated in our go bag.

"Okay, so you know how you complain every time the commercial comes on where the husband buys the wife a car for Christmas because it's financially irresponsible to make a major purchase of that size without consulting your partner?"

She turns around slowly. "There's also the one where the wife buys the matching trucks, one each, but I notice that's not the example you used."

I grimace. "Okay, so I signed the paperwork to have it delivered before those commercials started airing a month ago. It's a push present, and it's the blue Subaru Outback parked right outside the apartment front door."

"Hunter," she groans. I check my watch to see how long it's been since the last contraction. "No, that wasn't a contraction. That pain was solely caused by you."

I laugh, lowering my wrist. "Okay, I know, but here's the other surprise. We got the Safeway contract."

She drops everything she's holding to run, well waddle, forward as quick as she can to throw her arms around my neck. "You did?! Why didn't you tell me?"

"You know, push present, big romantic gesture, misguided man peabrain. The usual reasons."

She leans up and kisses me once before pulling away. "Okay, new house rule. Purchases four figures or larger have to be approved by the other party."

I bring my lips to hers again for another peck. "Engagement rings are the exception to that rule."

Michelle leans back, shock on her face.

"No, no. I don't have one of those hiding somewhere too. But wanted to write the exception into the house rule while we're in the negotiation stages."

Michelle's face contorts in pain as she grabs her side. "Okay, now that's a contraction."

I check my watch again. "Still six minutes apart. Let's say we get you to the hospital in a snowstorm, have a baby, and then we can finalize any new house rules."

"Deal," she says, heading for the door, everything she gathered in the last few minutes forgotten on the floor. I grab the go bag from the closet and follow her. My smile is indulgent. I'll worry about the mess my adorable girlfriend made later.

With the door behind us, I head to the stairs when I realize Michelle's not with me. I backtrack to find her standing just outside our door.

"You okay? Do we need an ambulance?"

She shakes her head. "No, no. I'm okay. The next time we walk through this door, we're going to be a family of three. I wanted to mark the occasion."

I pull her in a hug, leaning down to her ear and say, "I can't wait," before pulling back and finding a smile on her face to match mine.

"I'm a little nervous about the pain coming my way between now and then, but . . . me neither."

"All right then." I lace my hand with hers. "Let's do this thing."

I thank the parking gods who let me snag this spot a week ago when we only have to walk a few steps on the covered side-walk before I deposit Michelle into the car. My New England-self prepared for this storm by leaving the windshield wipers sticking up, but my snow-trained driving isn't prepared for a city full of transplants.

I blare on my horn for the fifth time in as many blocks.

"Relax, babe. We're going to make it." Michelle tries to soothe me.

"I don't understand why people are driving right now if they don't how to drive in the snow."

"Maybe they're all having babies too," she says, her tone telling me if I could take my eyes off the road to look at her, she'd be sticking her tongue out at me.

"You're lucky you're cute," I growl, navigating around a car with its four-ways on half in the lane and half in a parking spot.

Finally, I pull up to the hospital and run around to the other side again to meet the valet.

"Where did you grow up?" I ask the kid approaching from the valet stand, who can't be much older than seventeen.

"Uh, here?" he says, eyes wide, giving me an answer I've only heard a handful of times since I moved here in June.

I eye him warily. "Look, kid, the car is brand—"

"What he's trying to say is thank you so much for coming to work during a snowstorm." Michelle's voice comes from behind me. "You may not be able to tell, but we're about to have a baby and he's a smidge high strung."

The passenger side door is open and her feet are swung around, ready to touch the snow-covered ground. Decision made for me, I drop the keys in the kid's outstretched hand and rush to her side, helping her stand and step up on the curb.

Two steps later, Michelle stops walking, her face pinching in pain. She grips her stomach and breathes through the contraction. "I'd very much like to see a doctor and find out if it's time for drugs yet," she says. Her eyes open, her gaze surprisingly clear given the snow globe we drove through and what we're here to do.

"Anything you want, babe," I say. I wrap my arm around her back and guide her to the ramp leading to the emergency room entrance.

"Uh, sir?" the valet's voice comes from behind me, his voice indicating the last thing he wants to do is engage with me any further. "Do you need this bag?"

Michelle snorts a laugh. "Next time we have a baby, maybe a little less interrogating and a little more checking the backseat to be sure we have everything."

"Next time we have a baby"—I set her hand on the conveniently placed railing—"you're giving birth in summertime." I jog the few steps to the car and take a few extra seconds to log the valet's name. "Thanks for the heads up, Jack. I'll make sure you get a good tip whenever things aren't so pressing."

He nods, still looking like he'd very much like to get away from me. "Good luck, sir." Without another word, he heads to the other side of the car, and I move back to Michelle's side.

"You know, from a weather perspective, spring actually holds the least possibility of severe and sudden weather disasters," Michelle says as I approach. "But I do think we should see this one through before we start planning any more."

"Deal." Bag settled on my shoulder, I wrap my arm around her and continue our walk to the doorway. "You know, the valet kid called me sir twice." I mean to keep my tone nonchalant, but some of my surprise must slip through, because Michelle leans further into my side, causing me to look down at her.

"Fatherhood looks good on you, babe," she says, tilting her face up for a kiss. I meet her willingly, like I will every time she wants my lips on hers for the rest of our lives.

I check my watch and see it should be about time for another contraction. Grabbing a wheelchair from where a few are left unaccompanied by an empty security booth, I help Michelle settle into one. This seems like a time for forgiveness and not permission.

She grabs onto my hand firmly, breathing through the incoming contraction, right on schedule. A few seconds later, she opens her eyes, meeting mine.

"Let's go have a baby?" I ask. She nods, giving me her game face, determined to face labor head on. I move behind her so I can push us the rest of the way to the check-in desk.

"Though, if you want to take the first shift of pushing, I wouldn't complain."

"If I could, I would," I say, my voice earnest.

She reaches up to grip my hand and turns so she can see me while we wait our turn. "Love you," she says, her eyes displaying the depth of her emotion.

"Love you," I say back, intertangling our fingers on the wheelchair handle.

"Next," the administrator at the desk calls and I wheel us toward our future.

"Do you think if I renounce *Friends* as one of my favorite TV shows, the universe will stop giving me a Rachel-esque labor?" Michelle asks, squatting in her bed hours later. "I feel like I've been stuck at seven centimeters for longer than the night it took to make her."

I check my watch, trying to swim through the brain fog to do mental math. She may be on to something, but I assume an actual confirmation won't be helpful here. As tired as I am, I know Michelle must be at least three times as exhausted. She's having trouble getting comfortable, so I don't protest when she asks me to help her readjust to being on all fours.

A knock on the door catches our attention before Dr. Barber slips into the room.

"How are we doing in here?" she asks, sanitizing her hands and walking over to the bed.

"You know, I didn't do much yoga before getting pregnant, but the past few hours have me reconsidering. If I can do those poses in labor, surely I will rock it without a baby in the way."

Dr. Barber laughs, looking at Michelle's chart.

"You've been here almost as long as we have, Dr. B," I say. She hears the unasked question in my statement.

"I have been. With the snowstorm, our protocols change a bit, so I've been on duty for almost twelve hours. My relief should be here soon." Something flickers across her face.

"Who's coming in for you?" I ask, pretty sure I already know the answer.

"Dr. Jameson is scheduled to come in next."

A groan of pain leaves Michelle as another contraction kicks in. The doctor and I both start timing. After a minute, Michelle's body releases the tension, her breathing hard. I bring a cup of water with a straw close to her mouth so she can take a few sips of water.

"Can we hope the mention of his name alone kicked my body into gear? Because I would give almost anything to not have that fatphobic jerk deliver my baby." Michelle's eyes fill with tears.

I stroke her hair. "There has to be someone else here who can help. I'll find them." I promise. Seems even with our complaint, the guy has managed to keep his job.

"Let's get you on your back to so I can check your progress. If you go into active labor while I'm on the clock, I can stay to see you through," Dr. Barber says. She's doing her best to show a layer of professionalism, but I see her struggling to keep it in place. Seems like he's not very popular with his co-workers either.

She flags down a nurse, and we help Michelle navigate into position on her back. Michelle grips my hand while the doctor performs the same exam we've sat through countless times tonight.

Dr. Barber sits up, a large smile on her face. "Well, Michelle, good news. You're ten centimeters and fully effaced. Give me a second to gear up, and we'll start pushing."

A nurse hooks Michelle up to monitors, the room suddenly a flurry of activity, but her eyes are only on me. I bring my forehead down to meet hers.

"Hey, you're going to be great, okay? The climb to the very top of the mountain is here, but on the other side is our little girl. I'm so proud of you."

She nods her head, moving up and down against mine. "Sorry in advance if I crush your hand." A tear trickles out of the corner of her eye. I pull back slightly so I can wipe it away.

"Crush away. I can't imagine a better reason to need a cast."

"All right," Dr. Barber says, reentering the room, an air of assuredness around her. "Let's get ready to push."

Everyone takes their positions, and Michelle wraps her hand a little tighter around mine. "Next contraction in thirty seconds," a nurse says.

"All right, Michelle. When I say so, you're going to push as hard as you can. Are you ready?"

She takes in a deep breath, eyes closed, before opening them to a look of determination. "I'm ready."

Dr. Barber counts us down, and Michelle lets out a yell while she pushes down through her contraction.

"That was great, Michelle. I'm going to need you to be ready to go again, okay?"

Michelle nods, and I brush the hair out of her face, never feeling more invested and more helpless at the same time.

She pushes through the next few contractions, the toll and energy they're taking after a long night of labor clear on her face. A nurse appears out of nowhere, handing me a wet towel. Glad for something to do besides stand here and let nonsense praise tumble out of my mouth, I wipe sweat off Michelle's forehead.

"Okay, Michelle, I can see her head after the last one. A few more big pushes and we're going to have ourselves a baby."

Michelle nods, too exhausted to comment, but the determined look returns, stronger than before.

"Okay, the heads out, big push for the shoulders." Michelle screams again. "A little bit more."

The next noise that joins the room is the loud, screaming cry of our daughter. Michelle flops back against the bed, tears streaming freely down her face. I blink rapidly, finding tears spilling down my own face. They bring our daughter up to lay on Michelle's chest.

After a few minutes, someone says, "Dad, it's time to cut the cord."

I press a kiss to Michelle's forehead, and she squeezes my hand once more, with affection this time, as I step to where Dr. Barber holds my little girl, one half of my entire world. I follow the doctor's instructions and then watch as they take baby girl away to do the initial exam and clean her.

I take this brief moment to stroke my hand down Michelle's face, putting all the love and affection I can into my look.

"You were amazing. That's her, that's our daughter."

She nods. "That wasn't so bad, was it?" We both laugh wetly at the undersell of the past eighteen hours.

"Mom, Dad, here's baby girl Lewis." One of the nurses helps lift up Michelle's gown so they can lay our daughter on her bare skin once again.

"Hi there, baby," Michelle coos at the infant cuddled on her chest. My heart stutters with the effort to absorb all the love coursing through me while I gaze at the two most important people in my life. Michelle looks at me for a moment, and whatever she sees in my face helps her make a decision.

"It's baby girl Brandt," she says with finality, causing my heart to leap again. I already know they're my forever, but never assumed our daughter would share my last name from birth.

"We'll leave you three alone for a few minutes. You'll be able to start bringing family in within an hour or so." Michelle and I look at each other, confused, before looking at the nurse.

"Snowstorm or not, seems like you have some people determined to be here for you." She walks out of the room, smiling.

"Sounds like them to not wait for us to call like we said we would," I say, turning to Michelle.

She shrugs the shoulder our daughter isn't laying on. "I think your family isn't very good at showing they care from the sidelines. I'm not surprised they're here."

I laugh. "When you put it like that, I guess I'm not either."

We sit in silence for a moment, staring at the little human we created, changing our lives forever.

"I know we had our favorites list, and I'll call her baby girl for as long as we need to. But, any gut feelings?" I ask Michelle softly.

She gazes down at the tiny head with a smattering of red hair covering it before looking up and meeting my gaze. "I'm going to call an audible and throw out a Hail Mary," she says, biting her lip.

I roll my eyes. "Fucking Duncan for getting you hooked on those fantasy football podcasts. What's the name, babe?"

"Hope." She says the word simply, and in the second it takes for my synapses to fire and comprehend, I know it's perfect. Before Michelle, before that one night in March, my life coasted along perfectly fine. Because I didn't know what I was missing, what I could have once I found the perfect woman. And even when I didn't believe I deserved them, Michelle never lost hope I'd be the perfect man for her, the best father for our daughter.

"It's perfect," I breathe, scooting closer so I'm able to wrap my arms, however awkwardly, around them both.

"I thought so."

Another beat passes before I ask, "And the middle name we talked about?"

Michelle nods. "I think they go together perfectly."

"Me too," I say, and we lapse into silence, watching Hope breathe.

It's around an hour later, after the nurses have come and gone again, when another knock sounds at the door. Michelle and I look at each other and smile, before she says, "Come in."

Preston, Duncan, Hayden, Charlotte and Jax file in. "Look at her, she's so gorgeous," Charlotte says quietly, bringing her hands to her mouth.

"She amazing, guys," Hayden says. Preston and Duncan offering their agreement.

"Hold the phone up higher, Hay. I can't see!" Spencer complains, his face visible on a phone screen. Hayden complies and Spencer gasps. "Oh, look at her," he coos.

"Laurel told me the first thing I say has to be that she's pissed at you for going into labor while she's out of town and flights are canceled," Jax says, shrugging. "And I'll add she is absolutely beautiful."

Michelle laughs and shakes her head. "Here, Hunt, take her for a second? I'll send Laurel some pictures right now."

She lays Hope in my arms and my breath catches, like it has every other time I've held her this morning. Gathering myself, I walk over to where my brothers, both physically and digitally, stand.

"Hey, guys. I want to introduce you to someone. This is Hope Catherine."

Four identical gasps, one slightly delayed via phone speaker, fill the room when I say our mom's name following Hope. I glance behind me and see Jax and Charlotte, arms intertwined, their eyes glistening with unshed tears, while they stand next to Michelle's bed.

We stand there a moment more, the only audible sounds in the room intermittent sniffles.

Duncan finds his voice first. "It suits her. I know Mom would be thrilled."

"I think so too," I say, gazing down at my daughter. There's a lot that terrifies me about being a father. But I'm certain these people around me, faces so full of love for my little family, will help hold us up and never let me fail.

Epilogue

MICHELLE
Two weeks later

It's true what they say. Having a newborn is exhausting. But it's also exhilarating, life changing, terrifying, and fulfilling. See, exhausted and full of conflicting emotions.

As my brain comes online on Christmas morning, I see Hunter pulled the curtains open when he got up. Rolling to my right, I see the bassinet on my side of the bed is empty. Hunter must have grabbed Hope when he got up, wanting to let me sleep in a bit.

The cloudy skies make it hard for me to tell what time it is. A light snow is falling, and I hear faint sounds of Christmas carols coming from the kitchen. The reports don't call for a repeat of the snowstorm like the weekend of Hope's birth, thank goodness. Though, we don't plan to go anywhere—Hunter's family is all at his Dad and Margaret's place in Holly Ridge for the week. We're scheduled to do a video call with them later in the day.

I roll out of bed, making a quick pit stop in the bathroom to brush my teeth and throw my hair up in some semblance of a contained bun. The smells of breakfast wafting in from the kitchen make my stomach growl. Suddenly I can't wait to get out to my little family, to kick off this new kind of Christmas Day.

My quick steps are halted when I take in the scene in the kitchen. Hunter has on the same red and green plaid pj pants as the set I'm wearing. But instead of the button-down shirt on top, he has on a white tank top, tattoos on full display. Hope is plastered on his chest in the carrier, and as he turns to grab something from the fridge, I see she's wearing a bright pink body suit instead of her matching onesie. My heart warms as he moves around the kitchen as effortlessly as before, but now he's constantly aware of where Hope is and cautious he doesn't get her close to the hot surfaces.

"What happened out here?" I say, crossing to them and leaning up to accept a kiss from Hunter's lips before bending to place one on Hope's head.

"I'm worried your daughter isn't a fan of Christmas," he says, his eyes sparkling. "She did an exorcist impression all over my flannel top and her matching onesie."

"My *daughter* isn't a fan of Christmas?" I tease, walking into the living room to grab a small, wrapped package from under the tree, setting it on the coffee table. "I seem to remember several favors being promised to coerce you into putting on your matching pj's."

He removes a pan from the stovetop and turns to smirk at me. "You're the one who went to sexual favors immediately upon presenting them to me last night. I would have worn them because you asked, but if you were going to sweeten the pot, who am I to say no?"

I smack him on the ass before grabbing Hope out of the carrier and carrying her to the couch so I can feed her. "Butthead."

"Christmas-themed butthead," he calls back. "Do you want to eat in the living room when you're finished up?"

I unbutton my top and arrange Hope, who latches on almost

immediately. "Yes, please," I say while gazing down at her adorable face. I'm not producing as much milk as we'd like, so we're supplementing with formula too. She's gaining weight at a good pace, and it means we can share the nighttime feeding duty, which I know Hunter is thankful for. He loves middle of the night bonding sessions, resting Hope on his bare chest in the nursery's rocking chair Margaret got us.

For the next few moments, the only sounds are Hunter serving breakfast, the Christmas carols playing on the smart speaker, and Hope suckling on breakfast of her own. Contentment spreads through my veins. Me from a year ago would never have predicted this is how I'd be spending Christmas this year.

Hunter comes in from the kitchen, plates in hand, and stops next to the coffee table, gazing down at us with a proud smile on his face. "Every time I watch you feed our daughter, I can't believe this is my life." Apparently, I'm not the only one being sentimental this morning.

He sets the plates down on the coffee table and heads back for another trip. Hope's drinking slows and I bring her up to my shoulder to burp her. Seamlessly, Hunter lays a cloth under her head, so my pajamas have a chance of surviving the morning.

I nod to the plates on the coffee table. "Am I completely sleep deprived, or are those waffles shaped like Christmas trees?"

He brings the plate closer for me to examine and I see they are, in fact, Christmas tree waffles. "Found the iron on a middle of the night scroll about a week ago. We better hope this one's getting a scholarship, because I'm not sure how much college fund will exist by the time she starts sleeping through the night." His grin lets me know he's joking—I know for a fact Duncan opened a 529 plan for her the day Hope was born.

"Well, what a festive and fun addition to breakfast," I say, satisfied Hope's expelled as much gas as she's going to. I prop her in the pillow sitting on the couch between us, putting a Christmas waffle on the plate next to the omelet Hunter made, stuffed full of all my favorite things.

I moan around a fork full of eggs, cheese, bacon, and vegetables. "You know, I wasn't ready for how hungry breastfeeding would make me."

"You moaning makes me hungry for something else," Hunter says, and I meet his eyes, dark with want. "I'm still convinced Hope was conceived after I heard you make that noise over my eggs for the first time. Feeding you does something to me."

"Add it to the tab," I say, adding a little extra smolder to my gaze as I hold his. We both know he's all talk. He'd never dream of pushing me for sex before both the doctor and I say I'm ready, but damn if it's not going to be weeks of foreplay. When we're cognizant enough to recognize anything other than exhaustion, of course.

He exhales and shakes his head, cutting his waffle with a bit more force than necessary. The next time he looks at me, his eyes are simply full of adoration. "So, after breakfast, presents? Or should we save them to open on Zoom with everyone later?"

"Presents?" I ask. "I thought we said no presents given we had a baby two weeks ago."

Hunter looks with meaning at the packages under the tree and to the one I put on the coffee table earlier.

"Okay, the one on the coffee table is an extra onesie for Hope in the PJ pattern. I figured having a backup wouldn't be the worst idea. And most of those are for Hope from everyone, like we didn't have a baby shower a month ago."

He sets his empty plate on the table, talking as he moves to the tree. "Thank goodness she was born early and there's some space between her birthday and Christmas. No shared presents for our angel."

I laugh, knowing this girl will be spoiled rotten.

"But," he continues. "I did notice a few packages labeled 'To Dad, From Mom.' First, please always label my packages this way from now on. I had to sit down when I first read it. Second, you thought you'd be the only one to break the present rule and have something for me under the tree?"

I can't stop my smile from growing. "You're not the only one doing middle of the night shopping, I guess."

He shakes his head at me in mock scolding. "Well, you've been caught, Lewis. We'll save the rest to open with everyone else later, but I wanted to give you this while it's just us." He kneels on the floor in front of me and hands me an envelope with a bow attached. His chin rests on my leg, looking at me expectantly.

I slide my finger under the sealed edge and rip it along the fold. A gift certificate waits inside.

"A gift certificate for a tattoo?" I ask, after examining it for a moment. "That's really sweet." I say, meaning it, but confused why he couldn't give this to me in front of everyone else.

My expression must not do a good job of hiding my internal thoughts, because he chuckles. "I know. It doesn't seem like something private. You've mentioned you might want to get one someday, so I grabbed the certificate while I was in the salon for this." He leans up and pulls his tank top over his head, revealing a white patch taped over his left pec.

"That's why you've been wearing a shirt constantly the past few days," I say, my eyes bouncing between the square of white and his eyes. My emotions are still on a hair trigger, and tears well in anticipation.

"I may have been counting on exhaustion to keep you from asking. The artist I wanted left town for the holidays a few days ago. I got one of his last appointments for the year." His eyes lock with mine as he starts to peel away the tape.

My breath catches as the ink on his skin is revealed. Two line tattoos of flowers are centered, their stems intersecting with a jagged line representing the pattern of a heartbeat on a heart monitor.

"Are those . . ." my voice trails off.

"A violet for you, and a narcissus for Hope. Yes. Maybe a bit redundant to ink my heartbeat on top of my literal heart, but loving you, loving Hope . . . it feels like my heart beats on the outside of my body, because my chest can't contain all the love I have."

I lean down and press my lips to his, too overcome to form words. Instead, I push my gratitude, my love, through our kiss. The salt from my tears mixes in with the taste of Hunter.

"So, you like it then?" he teases once we break apart.

"I love it. I love you." I brush my hand through his hair, unable to stop touching him in this emotional moment.

"I love you too, Mich. Merry Christmas." He leans into me, his arms going around my waist, his head on my thigh. I wrap one arm around his shoulder, the other reaching to Hope. Not wanting to be left out of the moment, she wraps her little hand around my finger.

Soon, it'll be time to break the moment and connect with the rest of our family and friends. To celebrate the holiday with everyone who's come to mean so much over the past several months.

For now, I have everything I never knew I needed wrapped around me.

Acknowledgments

Authorship can be a lonely profession, but I feel so lucky to have an amazing group of people in my corner supporting me and lifting me up.

Thank you to everyone who has cheered me on during the writing of this book, or at any point in the last four years. I wouldn't be here without you.

Allie, Izzy, Kelly, and Steph - thank you so much for reading this one early and for your incredibly helpful insights and letting me know which lines hit home the best. Rachel, your support and cheerleading mean more than I can say.

Lacey and Cassie - thank you for sticking with me as I needed to move deadlines and for putting so much care into helping me make this story shine.

Ana - thank you for the cover of my dreams.

To all my online and digital author communities - this is a weird job, and I'm so glad to have found people who "get it."

To ARC readers and friends who shared posts and hyped this book up, I know Michelle and Hunter will reach more hands because of you.

And to you, dear reader - I wouldn't be here without you. Thank you for spending time with my characters and taking a chance on my stories.

About the Author

Rachel grew up in Western PA and found her love of reading early in life, supported by her parents with frequent trips to the library and local bookstores. She stumbled into the online bookish world in late 2020 diving headfirst into the Romance genre. In 2021, she changed careers and took a job at a bookstore and started her first official novel-length writing project.

Now Rachel is getting an MFA in Popular Fiction at Seton Hill University and juggling too many story ideas for one brain to handle. She's excited to continue to share Happily Ever Afters with you that bring the laughs and the love.

When not immersed in her bookish world, you can find Rachel hanging out with her husband and two cats, spending time with friends in the Washington DC area, and rooting for Pittsburgh sports teams.

* 9 7 9 8 9 8 6 5 7 6 2 7 5 *